Junie Smith
Experiences
Fear,
Memory Loss
and the
Movies

BY JANE KING

—

P.S. I hope you enjoy it.
Jane King

Galhattan Press

Galhattan Press
5 West 31st Street, New York, NY 10001

copyright 1994 Jane King
Galhattan Press first trade paperback printing

Printed in the U.S.A

Book Design: Charlene Benson
Cover image: Darryl Turner

for everyone who uses the telephone

———

"You'll call tomorrow?" Natalie begged or demanded. I wasn't sure which.

"Sure. Wait, wait a second. Tomorrow is Thanksgiving."

"But then it's even more important. You can call on Thanksgiving, can't you?"

"Yeah, I guess so. Okay."

It was my mother who originally told me to call her, or gave her my number, I can't remember exactly how it went. She was the daughter of people who lived down the hill from my parents in California. "What's her name?" I'd asked. "I guess her name is Natalie," my mother told me. "I'm not sure. I think it used to be Susan and she changed it. Her mother kept calling her Susan, but then when she introduced us she said 'Natalie,' even though it seemed like it cost her some effort. After the daughter was gone I asked, 'Natalie, that's your daughter's name?' as if I was just trying to remember, and her mother, Jeannie Johnson, sort of mumbled something like, 'Yeah, that's what she wants to be called these days.' She's coming to Chicago to work for a writer."

I was more interested.

"She's going to be his assistant," my mother said seriously. "He already gave her a full length sable."

Ah, that kind of assistant, I thought, though that made me no less interested.

The next morning I was awakened by the phone ringing.

1

"It's Thanksgiving," Wilbur said. "When are you coming over?"

As always, it excited me to hear him. "Pretty soon. What time do you want me?"

"As soon as you can get here."

I stood up, stretched, and looked around my apartment. It really was like living in a haunted house: ten rooms, the walls all covered with a thin coat of whitewash, cracks between the boards, and in each room a different color of faded linoleum. And why so many doors? I wondered. There were eight separate doors leading outside: two to the rickety outdoor stairway, two each to the indoor stairways on either end of the apartment, and two that just led into the air over the weed-covered lot.

I'd be happy to go up to Wilbur's much more normal house.

The phone rang again.

"June?"

"Oh, hi Natalie."

"I bought a turkey. When do you want to have dinner?"

"Um."

"You're coming over aren't you? You said so yesterday."

"I'm not sure. Wilbur asked me up to his place."

"But we talked yesterday. Please. You could come for a little while, we could have an early dinner, and then you could go over to his house. I'm lonely here." She lowered her voice to a whisper. "I can't stand to have Thanksgiving dinner with just Paul."

I could sympathize, but I was dying to see Wilbur and not that happy at being pressured.

"I don't know. I already promised Wilbur I'd go right over there."

"You could come for an hour, couldn't you? You could call him back and tell him you'll just be an hour late."

"But you can't make a whole dinner then have time to eat it in an hour—hour and a half, counting my travel."

"We could go out."

"Well."

"Please. I want you to come so much."

"All right." As usual, it was difficult for me to say no. I called Wilbur back. "Listen, I promised Natalie I'd go ever there for a little."

"Oh June. Why? What time will you come here?"

"Two hours."

"Two hours? I'm already waiting for you. I got some really great new videos at the store last night and I brought them home. *The Women*, have you seen that?"

"No, but I've heard of it. That's the one with no men in it, right?"

"Yeah, I figured you'd like that. Don't go there, June. Just come here. Call her back and tell her you'll be there tomorrow. I have to work tomorrow from eleven to four in the morning, that'll give you plenty of time to hang out with her."

"But I already told her I'd go. She's cooking a turkey."

"Did you say yesterday you'd go?"

"I don't think so—um, no, I didn't."

"Well, then, when did she buy the food? It should be okay anyway. She's got that guy hasn't she?"

"But she doesn't know him that well and she's homesick."

"But June, I want to see you. Call her back."

"Okay, I'll see you in a little."

"Great."

I hung up and called Natalie. "Listen, I don't think I can come."

"Why not? I already got started working. It's an organic turkey, too."

"I just promised Wilbur I'd spend the whole day with him."

She sounded totally depressed. "He won't even let me see you for an hour? Just come right over here now. Take a cab. I'll pay for it."

"Yeah, yeah. All right. I will."

I quickly put on my black coat and patent leather lace-up shoes and ran out the door (the right-hand one on the outside stairs). It was a bleak, gray day. I ran across the weed- and bottle-strewn front yard and down a block to Grand. There was little hope of getting a cab in this neighborhood. I kept turning around as I ran down the street, looking for buses so I could dash to the nearest stop if one was coming. There was no one else out. I was alone, surrounded by gray sidewalks, gray buildings, gray sky.

After six blocks the bus came and I got on, scrunching down into a seat near the wall and gazing out as the concrete industrial buildings slid by.

I got off on Erie and Michigan and walked over to her expensive high-rise. It was an old Chicago granite tower, massive gray blocks rising up, with griffins carved over the arched oak entrance. I announced myself to the ancient, militarily-dressed doorman. He smiled at me; I could see his dental bridge.

Off the elevator, I knocked impatiently on Natalie's door. I was wondering what I was doing here when I would so much rather have been about to see Wilbur's smile. (He'd start teasing me immediately, of course.)

Natalie and Paul lived in two apartments side by side, each with a shag-carpeted living room with huge windows, usually draped to hide their view of the lake, and modern kitchens, long halls (also with white shag carpet), and big bedrooms, two bathrooms in each. Between the apartments was a connecting door. Paul had specific ideas about closeness.

"June." Natalie smiled happily. "I can't tell you how much this means to me."

I could actually smell turkey cooking in the oven. "The turkey's been cooking for a while," I said.

"Oh yes. I was up at eight and had the turkey in the oven not long after."

"I'm sorry I won't be able to stay long enough to eat it."

Her eyes darkened a bit. "Let's go see Paul."

She knocked on the connecting door.

"Come in."

Paul slowly looked up. He had been running his fingers through his thick, white, rough-cut hair and it was standing straight out from his head. He had a black and gold pen in his hand. His elbows were resting on the small antique roll-top desk. He looked distracted.

Natalie hesitated. "Oh, pardon me. I thought you said you weren't working today."

"No, no, I'm not working. Just some personal correspondence. Please come in. Nice to see you, June." He smiled at me—I thought with just the tiniest hint of hunger, but then I was always imagining things.

It was much more than an hour later that I arrived at Wilbur's. He opened the door, but not with a smile. "You went over to her house, didn't you?"

I hung my head. "Yes."

"Can't you forget about other people for just one second?"

I didn't say anything.

"Well, I made you dinner. I don't know how it is now. It was ready a while ago."

We went into the kitchen and sat down at the table. I smiled at him anyway. I couldn't help it; he was so cute with his round Polish face, blue eyes, and convict crewcut. He was glaring at me, fighting his pleasure at my arrival.

"I'm glad you're here."

He took a slightly dried-out Stouffer's spinach soufflé and two plates with slices of turkey out of the oven.

"June." Natalie was whispering. **"I have to talk to you."**

"Why are you whispering?" I could hardly imagine that Paul was sitting right beside her in her bedroom.

"It's just too strange and very important."

"Okay."

"Can we meet?"

"Well, I don't know about today. I told Wilbur I'd make him dinner. He's got the day off."

"What about right now?"

"I'm trying to do the laundry."

"But it's very important."

"I dunno." I was reluctant to travel over to her house. It was such a nuisance to take the bus.

"Please, I'm begging you. I have no one else to talk to and I really am going crazy."

"Yeah, okay, but I can only come for an hour or so."

"We can't meet here. How about Sultan's on the corner?"

"Yeah, okay."

When I got there she was already sitting in one of the lavender plastic booths, drinking coffee and nervously tapping her toe. She used both hands to push her heavy black hair away from her face. I smiled a little as I slid in across from her.

"What's the story?" I asked.

"Great outfit."

I looked down. Yeah, I liked this one myself. Red painter pants, red t-shirt, and red tennis shoes. "Thanks." I looked back up at her.

"So? What is it?"

"Last night. Last night I went out."

"By yourself." This was not really a question. I knew Paul didn't like to go out.

"Yeah. Yes. That's part of the deal. I'm free to come and go as I like. He told me I can do whatever I want, but I'm, well . . . nothing dangerous. He's afraid of disease."

She was looking down in embarrassment.

I was sort of embarrassed myself.

"But never mind about that, that's not it—what I wanted to talk about—anyway. I went last night to the Raven Club."

"Yeah?"

The Raven Club had been an institution in Chicago since the beginning of time and possibly longer. It was small and traditional, with fake leopard fur seats and red flocked wallpaper. The stockbrokers—sleek modern versions of the old, florid, cigar-smoking stockyard owners—all hung out there. Everyone had a little experience under his belt and a lot of money. The bartender, Louis, was one of the men who set the odds for football pools.

Natalie pulled her shoulders in as she started the story. "Well, I just went for one drink and then I was going to go home, but after about half an hour the most gorgeous man in the world came in. He was Italian. Gino. Jeez, you should have seen the suit he was wearing. It was so elegant. I almost . . . Well, anyway, he was a real smooth talker, too. Right off the bat he told me he was married. But he hasn't slept with his wife in over four years. I guess she's an Italian Catholic and she doesn't want to get pregnant and ruin her figure."

"Yeah, sure."

"No, really, and he said I was the most exquisite creature he'd ever seen. He asked why was I in Chicago, he'd expect to find someone so precious in the Plaza Hotel in New York or leaning over the water on the Via Veneto. And his mouth . . . June, I could barely concentrate on what he was saying, you know, those full Italian lips. I mean, I was melting just watching them move."

"Yeah."

"Well, should I make a long story short?"

Usually I like long stories made longer, but something told me that this one was probably not going to contain charming offshoots like a ridiculous humiliating encounter with a celebrity or a new theory of time, and I did still have to do the laundry. "Yes. Short is good."

"He had a car, a gray Mercedes, parked in the garage around the corner—you know, right next to my building. And I was wearing my coat, did I tell you that part? Anyhow, we were making out. It was passionate, way beyond anything I have with Paul. Well of course, Paul's old and he makes me be so careful. Okay, so I might as well say it right out. Here's what happened." A note of hysteria crept into her voice. "He came on my coat."

I suppressed the urge to giggle. "What?"

"I told you. He got carried away. Oh, I was so angry. I yelled at him and we got out of the car right away, but it was too late. Oh June, help me! Tell me what to do. I could take you up and show you. I hid the coat in the back of the closet—not that Paul ever goes in there—but what'll happen when I wear it?

6

And what if I send it to be dry cleaned? I want to send it to the dry cleaner, but I've only had the coat for a month, for heaven's sakes, that would be totally suspicious, and you can really see the spot, it's right about here." She indicated a spot on her right hip. "You know, I can't hide it."

"Hmmm." I thought for a second. "Can't you just kind of crackle it off?"

"Yeah, I tried that a little bit. But it still would have been there. It's dirty."

"That's true. Well, I guess I don't know what you should do, I can't think. Is it okay if I mull it over and call you later?"

She looked disappointed. "But I thought you'd come up to the house and look at the coat."

"I can't."

"Please. You don't know how much this means to me."

Why on earth was I going to go do this? Go up to the luxury condo where she lived as the mistress of a romance writer to look at a come spot on her black sable coat? Why?

The truth is, right then I was in love with Wilbur, so the whole thing horrified me. I swear, when I have a boyfriend I am the biggest prude on the face of the earth. I cannot believe that people talk about sex, a sacred act performed in the intimacy of a love relationship. But as soon as I don't have a boyfriend, I mean *the very next day*, I talk about sex ceaselessly in the worst, most shameless terms.

Out to Dinner With Natalie and Paul

"Come out to dinner with us. Paul said he'd take us to Maxim's."

Of course I agreed. I wore my black cashmere sweater, tight because I'd accidentally washed it once, and a black skirt, black stockings, and high heels that were still in good shape—my friend Maria had given them to me only two months earlier. I met Paul and Natalie in the lobby of their building.

"I called a taxi," Paul said. He was wearing a tuxedo.

"My, my, you look great. I love men dressed formally."

He bowed. "Only fitting to escort two such young lovelies."

Natalie looked radiant, her black hair gleaming just a little more than the sable coat. Underneath she wore a black strapless dress, her flawless white shoulders contrasting with the silk.

7

The doorman nodded to Paul, then went and held the door. I could smell Natalie's perfume. Saint-Laurent. I knew it was expensive. We pulled up in front of Maxim's. The red-suited valet opened the door of the cab. I loved extending my leg out, the light catching the curve of my calf. In the restaurant the maitre d' bowed to Paul. "Mr. Henry, what a pleasure to see you again."

Paul smiled.

The room was dimly lit, with small shaded lamps at each table and here and there sparks of light shooting off from the movement of a diamond. The women were sharp-featured and elegantly coiffed, the men prosperous looking. We were seated in a round red leather booth, Natalie in the middle. I sighed with pure pleasure at the luxury.

The maitre d' bowed. "Your waiter will be here shortly."

Immediately was more like it. The waiter was standing in the maitre d's exact spot the second it was vacated.

"Can I offer you a cocktail this evening?"

We all ordered drinks; the waiter silently bowed and disappeared.

Paul smiled at me. "How do you like it here?"

"Yes . . . yes. I love it."

He beamed.

"You know the maitre d'?" I asked.

"This is one of my favorite places. Of course I'm not here so often, now that Natalie is feeding me nutritionally, but I have always enjoyed it."

"Look at that woman there." Natalie didn't point, but the direction of her gaze was obvious.

A large woman, in a gold lamé dress that covered her enormous breasts only just barely, was sitting with an extremely ancient, tiny man. Her hair was in a black bouffant and she was wearing impossibly long false eyelashes.

"Wow, that's wonderful," I said.

"You like her?" Paul looked around Natalie to me.

"Oh yes," I breathed.

"In what way?"

"You know, just to look at. She looks . . . extreme, and I like that."

"But you're not that extreme."

"I know," I said sadly. "I don't think I'm big enough for it. And I don't have the right looks. I'm better middle-of-the-road."

"I don't think I'd describe you as middle-of-the-road," said Natalie.

"Thank you." I bowed my head in semi-mock humility. "Now, I have to say, I *love* your looks, and you *are* more extreme."

"That's true," Paul said.

The waiter brought over menus.

"I don't believe I've met you before," Paul said to him. "I used to come here quite often not too long ago."

"That is true, I'm sure." The waiter smiled politely. "I've only been here a little over four months. My name is Paul."

"Well, my name is Paul Henry," Paul said.

"Look at her," Natalie whispered to me, nodding her head in the direction of a woman in a flesh-colored sequined evening gown, about eighty years old, with an oxygen tank beside her—she was smoking a cigarette. Many sparks of light flashed from her fingers as she brought her bony hand to her mouth.

We looked at the heavy green leather menus. There were no prices on mine. I ordered lobster, Natalie and Paul both wanted filet mignon. Paul also ordered a bottle of wine. I didn't hear what vintage he chose. Just like in my house, where I was taught that the girls weren't supposed to know anything about wine, nor should they ever touch the bottle—it's unladylike.

As Natalie and I looked over the other patrons, intently discussing them, we pretended to be completely engrossed in each other. We tried to laugh softly, but occasionally I burst out raucously. Paul listened and smiled, although he was not really interested.

When the waiter came to ask if the meals were okay, Paul detained him with a hand on his arm.

"Do you know who I am?" Paul asked the waiter.

"Certainly, sir, you're Paul Henry."

"Do you know what I do? Who I really am?"

"No, but it must be something very impressive considering the company you're keeping." Paul the waiter smiled now.

"I'm Dorothy Malone, the famous writer. Dorothy Malone. That's me."
The waiter looked confused.

"That's what I do." Paul's words were not slurred, but they were a little heavy. He had barely touched his dinner. "I write romance novels and I'm good at it, but my goddamn publisher insists that they won't sell without a woman's name. I have to use a woman's name. I'm Dorothy Malone."

"That's great, sir." The waiter looked anxious to leave. "I'll be back in just a minute." He poured more wine into all three of our glasses, then left.

The busboy came over to refill our waters.

"Do you know who I am?" Paul asked him.

"Yes sir, Mr. Henry. I've seen you in here before."

"Did you know that I'm famous as a writer of romance novels? Under a woman's name. Dorothy Malone. Did you know that?"

"Yes sir," the busboy said politely. "You told me, sir, on your last visit, and my wife was reading one of your books. She loved it."

For a moment Paul looked satisfied. He smiled. Then he frowned. "But it's terrible that I have to use a woman's name. I want to use my own name, Paul Henry. What's wrong with that?" He turned to Natalie and me. "Would you buy a romance novel by Paul Henry? You wouldn't care, would you, that it was a man?" He didn't wait to hear our answer.

"Don't pay any attention," Natalie said to me. "He always gets like this at dinner. What do you think of the redhead in the far left booth? Can you see her?"

The Movies Were Always There

"Good evening, miss," the doorman said and then waved me through, finally recognizing me.

I bounced on my toes impatiently, standing on the oriental rug in the hallway outside Natalie's door. I knew they had to look through the peephole before admitting me. Maybe it is the wealthy who are actually in danger.

The door swung open.

"Hold it for just a moment June." I heard Paul's voice. "Wait until I say before you come in."

I waited.

"Okay. But walk slowly."

I heard the whirr before I saw him with the movie camera held to his face. He walked backward as he filmed me. "I've been wanting to do this for quite some time."

"Does it have any sound?" I asked.

"No."

"Okay." I waved to the camera and smiled exactly as if I were a starlet from the 1950s.

Wilbur Objects

"I'm going to Natalie's."

"Why, June? You know I don't like it when you go over there."

"But you're going to be working, anyway. Why do you care?"

"I just don't like her. And that whole setup sounds bad. What kind of guy could he be that he would want a woman who could be bought? It's disgusting. Don't you have work to do? Writing?"

"Oh Wilbur, it's not exactly like that. She likes him and she's teaching him how to take care of himself."

"If a fifty-year-old man living on Michigan and Erie doesn't know how to take care of himself by now . . ."

Sometimes I couldn't believe how conservative he was. All I wanted was to go over and see what was happening. Their life was so different from mine. All that luxury, that was one thing, but even more fascinating was the relationship and what they were like as people. So foreign.

It wasn't nine o'clock yet when I arrived in front of the high-rise. I paced back and forth outside, wondering whether to buzz them even though I was early. Natalie had said between nine-thirty and ten. A silver-haired man walked hurriedly by, propelling a blonde in a fur coat and black pumps. Her hair was blown by the sharp wind. I pushed my hands deeper into the pockets of my purple suede jacket. I was cold despite the two cashmere sweaters I was wearing underneath. Only a short pleated skirt and wool tights covered my legs. I decided to go in.

"Good evening," the doorman said politely. Maybe he recognized me.

I smiled. "Paul Henry, please."

In the elevator on the way up I wondered how long I'd stay. I guessed I'd take a taxi to the club where Wilbur worked and just go home with him.

Paul answered the door. A blast of warmth rolled out and enveloped me. He seemed fuzzy.

"Come in, come in, we're watching TV in my apartment."

He led me through Natalie's living room and the connecting door, then past his living room study and into the overheated yellow TV room. I saw Natalie lounging on the gold-and-white sectional sofa, which went almost exactly from one edge of the 32-inch Sony television to the other, forming a square.

She turned heavy-lidded eyes to me. "Oh June, so nice to see you. We've been waiting."

11

I was puzzled. I was sure I was early.

My eyes went to the screen. I'd already gotten the impression that it was warm and golden. I couldn't quite figure out what was going on. Moving and smooth. The camera pulled back. WOW. My smile froze. They were watching porn.

"Please join us," Natalie softly said.

Paul was still standing behind me. "Yes. Please."

"I, uh . . ." I hadn't really been expecting this. My idea was to possibly drink a little Armagnac, listen to Natalie complain about what were to me the bizarre details of her life, then later leave and go to the dance club, where I felt at home.

Paul went over and sat down on the opposite end of the couch. Natalie patted a place next to her. She spoke slowly and carefully. "June, please, come sit next to me."

I walked around and sat next to her, feeling strangely hypnotized.

The porn was playing in soft pink, the bodies blown up, distorted, on the giant screen. The movie appeared to be about two girls.

"June." Paul said my name.

Suddenly I realized where this was inevitably leading. I was sitting very straight on the edge of the couch, my hands clasped before me.

"Well," I said forcefully and patted the couch on both sides of me. "I think I better go."

"Oh no." Paul sounded a little disappointed.

"I'm afraid so."

"If you have to." Natalie was slightly slurring her words, but she didn't sound unhappy that I was leaving.

"Please stay." Paul was sitting up very straight, looking at me.

I got up energetically and said in a cheerful voice, "I just can't. I have to go meet Wilbur." I walked around to the back of the couch where I'd been standing when I came in.

"I'll let you out." Paul reluctantly got up and walked me to the door. The taxicab to Wilbur's couldn't go fast enough.

(About five years later in New Mexico)

The thing with Mr. Sackler happened right before Christmas. I remember because I was thinking that the thief had been trying to raise money to buy his family Christmas presents and so I didn't mind so much.

When I worked at the country club there were certain gentleman members who would subtly make it known that if I were interested in being attached—in a house separate from-the-wife-and-a-vacations-in-the-Bahamas kind of way— they would also be interested, and I would equally subtly make it known that I was not that type of girl. It did intrigue me that the amount of time they took to notice me seemed to be proportional to their golf handicap. Always when I demurred it was perfectly civilized—I mean, we're talking about married men in their late fifties and early sixties, long past the tongue-hanging-out stage.

Once, though, when I dyed my hair blond—white blond—all the men who had crushes on me got completely out of control and began following me from room to room as I went about my duties. Now you have to imagine the country club, all low adobe and dark Spanish beams, polished wood floors. Out the windows was a view of the lush golf course with thickets of moss-covered willows. It was embarrassing to have a group of men standing and staring at me.

Mr. Sackler was one of the first and most persistent. I knew when it started. He was right in the middle of telling me about the promotion his son had received up in Denver and that he would probably be home for a couple of weeks—and he stopped in mid-sentence. I could almost hear him thinking, "Hey wait a minute, never mind that. Forget about trying to get her interested in Mark." But I quickly deflected the possibility of his asking the question. Waitressing is good that way, you can always run off.

He never really gave up. Every time he saw me, underneath his perfectly appropriate conversation, there was something else.

Once I walked up to him while he was eating breakfast on a Sunday. (I loved that shift—no bosses, just me and a couple of sleepy cooks in the far-off stainless steel kitchen.) He was sitting at a table with Mr. Goldstein and he asked me right out, "June, have you ever considered being kept?"

I was totally taken by surprise. "NO! No, I haven't!" I answered more sharply than was necessary. Both men looked startled. I could have answered the question as if it were a joke. He didn't ask any more direct questions after that.

Then one day—like I said, it was in December, right before Christmas—he saw me in the hallway to the men's card room.

"June," he said. "Listen, I have a friend who's looking for someone to rent his house, he's had to go to Los Angeles on business. Do you know anyone who might be interested?"

I thought about it. My friend Chase had recently moved in with me and we had discussed getting a bigger place. Also I had a crazy neighbor I was getting tired of.

"I might be interested. What's it like?"

"Pretty big—three bedrooms. It's out in the South Valley. He's renting it cheap for what it is, but of course you understand, he doesn't want me to give it away. What're you paying now?"

"A little less than two hundred. But I was thinking I might have a room-mate." By this point in the conversation I knew that we were actually discussing whether I would be kept.

"Would you like to take a look at it?"

"Yes. Yes, I would."

"How about Monday?"

"Of course, Monday would be great."

That was the day the country club was closed.

"How about meeting me at Ten Central Exchange around noon? Let's say twelve thirty. I'll buy you lunch."

"Okay."

Now, why in the hell had I agreed to meet him? I knew as sure as I knew my name was June that he wanted to pay me money to fuck him. Don't get me wrong, he was not an unattractive man—slim, in good shape, okay face, great black horn-rimmed glasses—but the question was, what was I punishing myself for? And I knew this was punishment because I was in therapy and I knew better than to think that prostitution is in any way healthy behavior. I discussed it with Chase and Clay and Rachel. It was possible that I just wanted money to move to New York. I also have this deep, deep, deep training to always be nice to people, especially men. I remember the time I was working in a corporation. I had been there about six weeks, my first business job, and one morning when I was taking the elevator up with the fifty-year-old man who was training me, he took my hand, smoothly pulled it over, put it in his pocket and massaged his penis. I said, "Pardon me," removed my hand gently, and never told a soul.

Well, this other morning, so many years later, I decided not to have sex for money but I didn't have any way of calling Mr. Sackler on the phone. I had spent the night at Rachel's so I got in my car to go down to my house and take a quick shower.

When I walked into the house, I thought, "I really have to clean this place up, it sure is messy."

Then I went into my office. "Something is missing here. What is it? Oh, the computer. Hmm, where is it? Did I lend it to one of the neighbors? No. I've been robbed." The information hit my conscious brain at the same time as a huge wave of extreme excitement. I threw my arms up in the air and yelled. "I'M RICH! I'M RICH! I'M RICH!"

I had great insurance and everything was gone. Wow. It was the most fabulous thing. All the useless, half-functional electronic objects would be replaced with money. Wow. Then I remembered my date with Mr. Sackler. Fuck. I changed my clothes and got into my beat-up Ford and sped down to the restaurant.

He was there, along with many of the more regular country club members— the men who had so much money they didn't need to work, who hung out in the men's card room playing poker and drinking bourbon, whose shifty eyes would slide past you when you waited on them, wondering what else you would get for them. Obviously these men all came here when the club was closed. Among them, getting drunk, was Amadeo, the bar manager who wished with all his heart to be a crony (and never would be) of the white, moneyed members. I was kind of embarrassed. I mean, why else would I be meeting Mr. Sackler except for an assignation?

"Sit down, June. What would you like for lunch?"

I had soup and a club soda, too happy for food. He had a roast beef sandwich.

"Are you ready to go see the house?" he asked.

"Oh, yeah," I said as if I had forgotten, whereas in truth my mind had been doing the wire rat-run the entire time. Should I go? Shouldn't I go? Should I?

We walked to his car and got in. It smelled slightly of dust.

We drove about half a block.

"Listen," I said. "I'm worried. Maybe I don't want to go see the house after all." My mouth was dry.

"We can turn back if you want." He didn't move. His eyes stayed straight, looking at the road.

"Well, I think the house is probably too expensive for me."

"If you think so. I guess the house *would* be too expensive." He said this with a slight sneer, a dare, as if saying to me, "Okay, all right, if you're not brave enough."

I didn't care. "Yes, I'd like to go back to my car."

We had only gotten about one block away, so it was a matter of seconds before I was unlocking my car and driving away.

(More time has passed)

"What's been going on with you?" Clare asked. Clare had been my best friend in Chicago, I'd met her through Wilbur. Clare was a deeply empathetic social worker. She had short straight hair and a round face with curiously down-turned eyes. She was only pretty when she smiled.

"Well . . ." I paused. "It's been a long time since we talked, hasn't it?"

"Yeah, I think it was before Christmas. You were excited about that guy who was going to maybe help you with the book."

"That's what's been going on. I rewrote the book for him and he told me he hated it. He said he'd given it to a friend of his who'd also hated it. Then he said, 'Why didn't you tell me you were Irish? Why do you hide it? If my friend'—whatever his name was, I can't remember, Sean McMurphy or something like that—'if he'd known you were Irish, he'd've loved the book.' Now what kind of bullshit is that? The guy doesn't like the book unless I'm Irish? Anyway I'm not Irish, I'm fucking American."

"You sound mad."

"That's not the worst of it. After he'd completely insulted me, it turns out that he'll still help me." I made my voice exaggeratedly sweet. "He still *wants* to introduce me to his best friend, the president of Penguin American, but I have to be his girlfriend."

"He said that directly?"

"No, no, not directly, but that's what the story was."

"You sort of suspected that all along though, didn't you?"

I felt sad, defeated. "Yeah, yeah, I did. I always do, but this time I hoped. He did read the other book and said he liked it. I always hope."

"I'm sorry."

"It's worse, even." I paused and almost sighed. "You remember I wrote you about that guy who was a senior editor at *Entertainment Weekly*, Aaron? He also told me he would help me. He also read the book and it was the same thing."

"What?"

"He would help if I would be his girlfriend."

16

"Aren't you speaking euphemistically? Girlfriend, is that what they wanted? You could just say they wanted to fuck you."

The remark stung me. "No, no. Not a one-night sex thing. They wanted me for a long time. They both suggested I should live with them."

Clare was apologetic. "All right, maybe you're right. Maybe it was girl-friend."

I didn't answer for a second, savoring my own displeasure at men. "I'm completely and totally annoyed. You can't even imagine what this has done, pushed me right over into radical feminism. I'm hoping this is only a stage because as things stand I'd just as soon spit on a man as . . . Oh my god, I can't believe I said that, that's so unlike me, I was going to say, 'as kiss them.' You know, I believe that for men—and this is not a surface thing, it is very deep—women are on about the same level as *cows*. On the surface, sure, right, it's cool, they're liberated, women should get the same salaries as men which actually I do not for one fucking second think they believe when it comes to THEIR OWN salaries. BUT . . ." I paused. "Where was I?"

"You were at the part where women are the same as cows."

"Yeah, right, that's right. And they all think it. They can't help it, it's in the culture, they learn it when they're born. They probably start learning it when they're still in the uterus."

"Who teaches it to them in the uterus?"

"Their mothers, that's who. Women are just as responsible for this whole fucking mess as men."

"I agree with you there."

"And the sad thing is, I don't think men like it any better than women. The problem with having all the power is that you also have all the responsibility. I think men are angry that they have all the responsibility."

"Right. And most women, all they want is to marry a rich man."

"Me. I want that," I said.

"So you won't have to be responsible," Clare responded quickly.

"Right. Exactly."

"Well, you're right about all this," Clare teased. "So are you marrying a rich man?"

For the first time, I was amused. "I guess I might have to get rid of that idea if I'm going to be a radical feminist."

Sam the Artist at Home

He lumbered across the room and got into bed, a futon raised on a platform. He smoked a joint. He brushed back his long greasy blond hair with a thick hand.

On the side between the bed and the wall the dirty clothes made a pile not quite as high as the mattress. He reached over to the bedside table and got the remote control. Four ten in the morning—he'd missed only the beginning of the late movie. *On the Waterfront*, yeah, there was Brando lurking in the shadows. Good. Yeah, good, and there was an unopened bag of potato chips on top of the fridge, he'd get them when he finished his cigarette. He looked in the pack—five left, more luck. They'd last until after morning coffee.

Clare #11

I was lying on my bed, doing my homework. I was wearing blue sweat pants and no top.

My friend Clare called. "June?"

"Yes?"

"I want to . . . umm . . . oh, wait, how are you?" Her sentences were always delivered staccato.

"Fine, I'm fine. You know, New York is crazy, but everything seems to be going right along. How about you?"

"Well, that's why I called. I'm thinking of calling Sam on the phone to see if I could go over and look at his artwork. What do you think? D'you think he'd remember me?"

"Didn't you meet him a bunch of times?"

"No, only twice. Or once, really. That time you took me over to his studio to see the paintings and we talked a bit and the other time was when I dropped you off when you were visiting, but that doesn't really count because it was just for a second, I never even got out of the car."

"Right, yeah."

"So you could see how I would not exactly be sure that he'll know who I am."

18

"Well, you could just explain it, I think. I'm sure he'd be happy. You know, he's an artist, so he loves to talk about his work. Much more than he likes to do it."

"You're sure about that?"

"Really, I swear, I'm absolutely totally positive. Sometimes I read articles about artists who claim that they don't like to talk about their work, they just do it, but that's not any of the artists I've ever met. Anyway, if you remind him I'm sure he'll remember you."

"Okay, well, I'm not going to talk longer. You know, my phone bill last month. Of course if you had something to tell me . . ."

"No, no. That's okay. My life is just going along."

"Well, then, I'll call in about a week or so to report what happened."

Clare on the Other End of Town From Sam

She squinted at herself in the mirror, then smiled real big, fake. She looked better when she was smiling—her laugh lines were hidden, her eyes turned up. She put on her cat-eye sunglasses and smiled again. Now she looked extremely good. A little like a bug with the thick white frames, but very, very sexy.

Maybe it was stupid, this date, asking him out. Her friend June said it was okay, said he would never even suspect it was a date, but still. She squinted at herself again, went over to the full-length mirror on the back of her bedroom door to look at her outfit. Long red cotton sweater, black leggings, red suede slippers. It was good. She did have good legs, she had to admit. She swiveled sideways suddenly. Still good. Okay. It would be fine, he wouldn't think it was a date. What else had June told her? "Talk about his art, he loves that. If he asks you anything about your romantic life confess a weakness for men much younger than yourself." Clare had giggled at this point. June had interjected sternly, "Well, it's true, isn't it? But completely refuse to divulge any details."

While Playing the Kidney Bean in the First Grade Play,
Secrets Are Revealed

"Clare?"
"Yes?"
"Is this too late?"
"No, no. Wait a minute. Let me get to the other phone."

I imagined her apartment had not changed since I'd been in Chicago, the dark wood floors, the striped material that she had not yet figured out how to turn into curtains tacked onto the windows. The deep purple couch and beside it, on a table, a Chinese bowl filled with objects she thought might interest guests—Maori charms and porno playing cards from the fifties, a plastic screw with threads running both up and down, a puzzle box.

I never could understand what phone she was changing to. Did she answer in the kitchen, her tiny neat kitchen with the best specialty coffee beans in the freezer and the amaretto on top of the refrigerator, then move to the bedroom? Or was she sleeping and, since we would probably talk for awhile, move to the dining room? Maybe that was it. I know she often painted while we talked.

"How's it going?" I asked.
"Pretty good."
"So, tell me, what about the thing with Sam?"
"Oh, yeah, well . . ."
"Well what?"
"We went out on a date."
"Really? Already? Wow. How was it?"
"You know, it was great."
"Great? You mean you called him and you've already gone on a date and it was great?"
Clare laughed. "Okay, you know, to me any sort of date would look wonderful, but objectively, it was good."
"So what happened?"
"Well I called him just like you said. I don't think he remembered me, but he was quite nice and we had a good time talking. We talked for two hours."
"Two hours? Wow. When was this?"
"Last Friday night."

"Okay, go on."

"He said maybe we should meet, or remeet, and I said that would be fine with me. He called back on Tuesday and we talked for two hours again, or I think maybe two and a half. Then he said he'd call on Wednesday and he did. About 7:30. He asked if I'd like to go to dinner and I said sure. You know, it seemed a little redundant because I'd agreed the day before to go out with him. Of course I could have changed my mind . . ." Her voice drifted off, as if she were talking to herself. "Or maybe he was just being courteous—yeah, that's it."

"Yeah, so . . . Tell me, already. What happened?"

"Oh right. Umm, well his car didn't work, the transmission was acting up, so I drove down there and he asked where I wanted to eat, but before I could actually say, he told me there was not much but Mexican restaurants."

"But wait. Doesn't he live near that street where all the Italian restaurants are?"

"Oh, you're right. I didn't even think of that. To tell you the truth I wish I'd remembered. I wasn't in the mood for Mexican food at all."

"But you had a good time?"

"Oh yeah. You know, Sam is not my physical type at all, but he really is intelligent and he has some interesting ideas."

"So how'd you leave it?"

"He was complaining about how his opening was next Thursday and he wished he had a bathtub, so I asked him over for dinner and a bath and he accepted."

"Yeah, that's good."

"He was so funny. He offered to bring Mexican food. I said that I thought I'd be able to manage cooking a meal. I didn't know if I'd be able to manage anything else, but the meal part I had down."

"What time?"

"I said sevenish."

"Don't get worried if he's late."

"Oh. You think he'll be late?"

"He might be," I said. "You know, I've known him for a long time and I'll tell you. He can be late. It's just like that other thing that I told you—how he'll never call you. Remember? How he never calls anyone, even though he sincerely means to, it's just that he forgets until so much time has gone by that he's embarrassed."

"So you think he'll be late for sure."

"No, not for sure, but maybe."

Clare sighed. "I guess I'd better not worry about it ahead of time."

"What else is going on?"

"Hmmm. Do you remember me telling you that I had this one client that I really adored, this guy Brian? He's always tried to play tough, but actually he's the sweetest kid in the world."

"What else did you tell me about him?"

"I've been seeing him for a long time. His foster mother couldn't handle him, said he was evil because he wanted to hang out at the Laundromat. Maybe I told you the story of how once one of the other kids said I was too skinny to fuck and Brian wouldn't tell anyone why he beat the kid up. Of course he was going to get punished. Then during our session I asked him, and he started crying and it all came out. To him it was so horrible what the other kid had said, he wouldn't repeat it even to get himself out of trouble. And you know, the fact that he was defending me just melted my heart."

"Yeah, I remember that."

"Well, I have to admit I'm a little sad about this. He's being transferred to Detroit. An earlier foster mother said she'd take him back."

"I'm sorry."

"There's nothing I can do. From what Brian's told me about her I'm pretty sure she just wants the money, but we're overcrowded as it is and the state naturally jumps at an opportunity to place a kid. I'll miss him, though. He's just about, well, I shouldn't say that, but I think he's adorable. I'll miss him. But that's enough. What about you? What've you been doing?"

"Not much. Going to Columbia. Working all three jobs. One of my fellow students was over the other day, very good-looking guy. I had my regular glasses on, my hair back, clothes covered with Ajax. I was scrubbing the floor while he tested me on my French vocabulary and he started begging me to have an affair with him. 'Dave,' I said. 'Really, the idea is great. But I just can't. I'm too tired."

"June, you are amazing. Where do you find all these men?"

"It's easy, Clare," I said. "I just think they exist."

I Call Her

"June?"

"Naturellement."

22

Clare laughed. "I suppose you're calling to find out how the second date went."

"Hey, let's not waste time."

"Great. It was great. He came over at about eleven o'clock. I was painting. You know I always feel stupid telling him I paint, though I'm dying for him to be my friend for that reason alone. So he can maybe critique me or show me techniques, or—oh, I'm not sure, but it's kind of a dream of mine. I don't know, though, this particular evening I didn't mind that he was looking at my work. I was just humming and puttering around. I asked him if he wanted an amaretto coffee and he said yes. I got that, put a towel in the bathroom, started the bath and went back to painting. Then I noticed he looked a little worried. 'What is it?' I asked. 'It's stupid,' he said. I had to coax him to tell me, then finally it came out. He was worried that maybe my bathtub might be too small, in which case he couldn't use it."

June laughed.

"Oh no," Clare chided. "He explained to me that it could happen. Once in Seattle he evidently had a horrible time in a bathtub that was too small. He got stuck." She giggled. "I took him in and showed him the bathtub. You know, without laughing. Then when he said it seemed like it'd be okay—I mean, you know my bathtub, it's huge—I turned on the water and asked him if he'd like another amaretto coffee and of course he said yes."

"Then what happened?"

"Well, pretty much what you'd expect. He took a bath." She giggled again. "Men are so cute, aren't they? After his bath he went right in and lay on my bed. Then when I didn't go in right away, he wrapped the towel around himself and came out looking for me. I told him to just relax, I'd be in in a minute, there were just a couple more things I needed to finish."

"So you slept with him?"

"Well, yes, I did. I have to admit that after acting so casual, I rushed through the things I had to do. After all, it's been, what? Three years since I had a lover of any sort. No. Three and a half."

"Damn." I had never liked enforced celibacy, even the idea. I thought sex was a natural function. Giving it up made about the same amount of sense as giving up breathing. "What happened the next day?"

"The next day was his art opening and so he had to leave pretty early in the morning. I knew I was going to see him later, of course. He was pretty nervous about the show."

"Yeah, Sam is always convinced everything is going to go wrong."

"I got a new patient."

23

"Wha, what who, wha, wait. Hold on a sec. You're not going to tell me about the opening?"

"You want to hear about that?"

"Brother."

"Normal. Pretty normal. Sam was completely obsessed with what he was wearing. You're going to have to help him when he comes to New York. I didn't tell him, but it *is* true you shouldn't wear white pants with a heavy gray wool sport jacket, particularly in December. I just calmed him down. By the time I got to the gallery, there wasn't anything he could do about it, so I just assured him he looked fine. I looked around at the show. He was right, those aluminum frames he made were perfect and I told him so. I said that when he was making them I was kind of skeptical about whether they were worth killing himself for, but now that I saw them I had to say he was right. Luckily my friend Albert showed up. Accidentally. He was just out gallery-hopping. I don't know if you'd remember who he was, I supervised him on the unit last summer when he was doing his internship. He's very good-looking and we had a great relationship so I was happy he was there. You know what I mean. It didn't hurt for Sam to see me hugging a handsome younger man."

"Uh huh. Right. Yeah."

"Then we all went to dinner. At first I didn't know if I was invited, but I started to say good-bye and Sam looked at me like almost hurt, as if I was deserting him, so I said, 'Well, I just didn't know if I was invited.' He said, 'Of course you're invited. You're my date.' His dealer Kenny was there."

I interrupted, "His dealer is a man?"

"No, Kenny is a woman. I dunno, the name must be short for something. Kendela, Ashkendra, Dukena . . ." She laughed. "Okay, what was I saying? Ah, the attendees. Also Janis—you know, the older woman who was his girlfriend for a while. He won't tell me anything about it, but I know he slept with her. She's very polished, with blonde hair, very done up. And this young girl who works at the gallery, Heather. I think she has a crush on Sam. Then there was Kenny's boyfriend, and one of the other artists, Billy something. I forget. Right before we left, Kenny showed me one of Billy's paintings in her office. He isn't very good."

"So dinner went okay?"

"I think so. I talked to Kenny and Janis. I think I did okay. We had a lively discussion of art magazines' preference for New York artists."

I laughed. "They can't help it. Those are their friends. It's natural to like your friends' work better."

"It's just frustrating if you live somewhere else," Clare said.

24

"Okay, speaking of frustrating, what about your job and that new patient?"

"Oh my god. Get a load of this. It's a sixteen-year-old kid. He's been in all the newspapers, but not with his name of course. He shot his aunt and uncle, who were his legal guardians."

"Jesus. Did they die?"

"No, and this is the wildest part. They both lived. He shot his aunt in the head and arm, both turned out to be superficial wounds. But his uncle almost died. This all happened about six months ago. He just got moved to our unit. I saw him for the first time last week, and today I saw the aunt and uncle. So I was trying to find out how angry the uncle was and I said to him, 'I guess you must be pretty angry at Joseph.' And he said, 'Oh, no, we're not angry at all. We feel sorry for him.' Isn't that incredible? The strongest case of denial ever. Someone shoots you in the stomach and almost kills you when you've been taking care of them and you're not angry. Yeah, sure."

"That is unbelievable. What about the kid? What's he like?"

"You know. Fucked up, shaved head. Trying to act tough. That's how all these kids are and underneath they're so scared."

"Jeez Louise, that's crazy. How'd you get assigned him?"

"That's not all. I got a collect call from Brian, you know, my kid who moved to Detroit. He wanted to come back."

"Can you do anything?"

"It's difficult. I went to my supervisor, Mary. I've told you about my little encounters with her. She's very closeted."

"Yes."

"I asked her off the record if there was a way to have Brian transferred back to the adolescent unit here, but evidently there's no way." She sighed. "I knew that. The state is about to merge the unit with a men's unit from the South Side. They're closing that facility down."

"Oh my god, that's terrible, right?"

Clare sighed. "Yeah, the boys we have now are mostly just confused. If you treat them like adults and aren't afraid, it's okay. I had a little guy who came in yesterday. He's thirteen years old, he has 666 badly shaven into his hair. He was telling me he could beat up anyone on the unit and they were all pussies and I just listened—'Uh, huh, yes, I'm sure you can, and when he was finished I asked him if he missed his sister and he burst into tears, confessed to me that the thing he felt the worst about was deserting her. You know, they're not bad kids, just tremendously scared."

"Scarred?" I misunderstood.

She laughed. "Yeah, that too. Scarred and scared."

"Oh my oh my oh my. Well, I'll be interested to hear how this goes."

"The kid?"

"Well, you know, the kid and Sam both."

She laughed. "Okay. I guess we better hang up now. Last month I got an atrocious phone bill."

"Okay, we better go."

"Oh no, wait. Did Sam call you?" Clare asked.

"No, uh uh. Why would he?"

"You remember he's coming to New York at the beginning of January for his show there. I think he's planning—or hoping, I should say—to stay with you."

"Well, if he calls I'm just going to pretend that's the first I heard of it."

"Yeah, great, okay. Good thinking. I think you're right about that. Talk to you later."

Sam Comes to New York

Sam called finally to tell me he was coming for that opening and asked me if maybe he could stay at my house. He was arriving on Thursday. I told him that if he called me at work I'd give him directions and meet him at home. When the doorbell rang I had just finished boiling water for tea, outside it was raining—hard, cold sleet. Sam's hair and the top of his canvas suitcase were wet. I laughed seeing him trudging dolefully up the fourth flight of stairs.

"Sam." When he got to the landing I gave him a hug. "Come in, I've just made tea."

My apartment was small, but warm, and the floors were golden wood.

"Here." I gave him a towel for his wet hair.

"I wasn't sure exactly where you lived so I had the cab driver drop me on the corner. I walked the wrong way. I guess I'm nervous about the opening tomorrow. Oh, that reminds me. I better hang up my jacket now."

He unzipped the suitcase and took out a wrinkled brown tweed jacket. He hung it on a hanger over the bathroom door and brushed it with his hand. "There. It'll be okay, don't you think, by tomorrow? June, I need your help dressing tomorrow. I brought this jacket. I think it's okay, but I don't know what artists wear in New York."

"We can worry about that tomorrow. You can show me the alternatives and

I'll tell you what's best."

"Will you?"

"Yeah, sure, of course. Want tea now? I think it's too wet for us to go out."

"Oh yeah, that'd be great."

I served the tea. He was sitting in the blue wing chair, I was sitting on the windowsill. There wasn't much furniture in my apartment. "So how's it been going?"

Sam frowned. "Good. Yeah. I've been exhausted doing these two shows together. I don't think I've had more than three hours' sleep for over three months, but I did get it all mostly done, all except one more thing I wanted to try on the aluminum frames but I had to give it up. June, you don't know how worried I was. A month ago I barely had enough paintings for the Chicago show. I'm a wreck."

"Maybe we shouldn't go out tonight then. We could hang around and talk, then you could sleep. You can sleep on the bed anyway, and I'll sleep out here."

"Awww, June, you don't need to do that. I can sleep out here."

"No, no. I wouldn't hear of it, you know I have the foam roll-out, and it's okay for me because I remain absolutely motionless while I sleep, whereas I don't think you do."

"You mean you remember." Sam alluded to our past.

"No, just a guess." Irritated, I denied it. "Based on my knowledge of your personality. Tell me, what's been going on besides working ten million hours a day?"

Sam almost smiled, but not quite; he squeezed his tiny eyes shut a little more to indicate amusement. "Well, you know I've been trying to buy this building."

"Oh, yeah, that's great."

He looked out the other window. "I've been kind of dating Clare."

"Huh?" This was some kind of automatic reaction, I wasn't trying to pretend like I didn't know.

"Your friend Clare. Didn't you know?"

"Oh, yeah, of course I knew." I shook my head as though to shake out confusion. "I don't know what that was. Anyway, I guess I talked to her a month or two ago, she said she went to your studio and you were going to come for dinner."

He breathed a sigh of relief, possibly that we hadn't been discussing his sexual prowess.

"I went on a date with her. Well no. It wasn't a date. We're just friends. She had me over to dinner a couple of times."

I pretended disinterest. "Yeah, so you're friends. That's good."

He looked at me cautiously. "Well, we're a little more than friends."

I acted surprised. "You are?"

"Yes, but I'm not interested in her. Well, I am and I'm not. I'm attracted to her, but then sometimes I'm not. I don't know. It seems like being around her is a lot of work. I don't know what will happen next. She seems to be uncontrollable."

"Hey, that's what Wilbur used to say about me. Even his best friend Al gave that as the reason we broke up one time. He said exactly that—I was uncontrollable. And I said, 'Who wants a girlfriend they can control?'"

"Yeah, but it's different with you, June. I'm not afraid of you. I'm afraid of her."

"Why?"

"I don't know."

"So you slept with her?"

Sam looked ashamed. "Yes."

"Was it okay?"

"Yeah, it was a lot of fun. She let me take a bath in her bathtub, too, and you know how I feel about that. She has a big bathtub."

I laughed. "Yeah, she does." Then I sighed. "I don't know. I'm completely pissed off at men myself." I looked at him slyly out of the corner of my eye so he would know not to take me too seriously. "I had two guys offer to help me with books if I'd be their girlfriend."

"Really?"

"Yeah. I don't know, the whole thing is so fucked up in my opinion. I was talking to this woman I met in California, a friend of my mother's. Younger than my mother, but they were going to college together. Somehow we got on the subject of men." I laughed. "Unbelievable as that may seem."

"No, no sirree, I can't for a second imagine you talking about that." Sam rolled his voice around the words.

I ignored him. "So she was telling me that her first husband refused to fuck her after they got married. Like, starting on the honeymoon. It's called the 'I do' syndrome. It's common. Evidently, as soon as the man gets married he assumes the role of his father and the wife must be the mother, and because he wants so strongly to imagine his parents have never been sexual, he would be a bad husband if he still slept with her. Well, then I told her that I had a boyfriend once who punished me by not sleeping with me. My boyfriend thought I was having affairs, which I wasn't, so he refused to fuck me. And then I told her I thought . . ." I was talking very excitedly and a little loud.

Sam looked besieged. "Yes?" He cocked his head to the side to indicate that

I was perhaps being slightly melodramatic.

I smiled and calmed down. "Well, I thought that was it. It was over. I would never get to have sex again. I was twenty-nine. I figured that no one would ever be attracted to me again."

"And now what have you learned?"

"I've learned that people still want to fuck me, but if I talk to them for longer than about half an hour, I'm completely horrified by what's in their souls so I never get laid anyway."

"Never?"

"Pretty damn close."

"But June, you could get laid a hundred times a day if you wanted to."

"You know the problem Sam. I can't just fuck anyone. I'm a dead serious person."

He laughed. "That you are."

The Next Day

"Good morning."

"Sam, I'm hungry for chocolate."

"For breakfast?"

"Well . . . anyway, it's almost eleven o'clock. I know where we can get the most perfect truffles."

"Okay."

We spent the afternoon sitting on the floor, eating chocolate and reading magazines.

"How're you going to dress for the opening?" Sam asked me.

"Sex goddess."

He laughed. "You'll never change, will you?"

I knew. I always knew what Sam thought of me. Once he'd said to me, "You know, you'd do allright, June, if you'd just stop looking for a pretty boy." And my taste in music—boy, did he think that was a clear indication of my character. Pop. Dance music. Sam thought it was obvious I was only interested in surface.

I had asked my friend Eileen if she wanted to go to the opening. She was going to come meet us at the house. A couple of minutes before she was supposed to arrive Sam stopped worrying about his clothes long enough to ask what she was like.

"Pretty," I said, then paused. "Very pretty and very fucked up. I wouldn't go anywhere near her if I were you. She's young. Just gave up drinking, so I hang out with her sometimes. She might be a writer. Anyway, don't worry about talking to her. I highly doubt she'll talk at all."

He frowned.

Eileen rang the bell.

"Are you ready to go?" I asked him.

"Yeah."

"All right, then let's just go down."

We walked the four flights. I introduced Eileen to Sam in the cramped stairway between the first and second floor.

Sam squinted his eyes the tiniest bit, in appreciation, I knew, of her red hair and lovely fair skin.

"This is the first time I've ever met anyone from Chicago," she said.

It was cold and snowing lightly. The streets were filled with people also on their way to important social events.

"It's inside one of those big buildings on Broadway," I said. "You'll see, there'll be a lot of openings tonight and we can go to all of them. Actually the thing I like the best is the floors. Those huge open spaces with gleaming wood floors."

When we got to the gallery, it was empty except for Sam's new paintings. Multi-hued heads composed of tubes, snakes, strings twisted into shape. Tortured machines trying to become human. They all looked to me like the feeling you get when you promise yourself that this time you won't yield to an addiction and then the next thing you know LO! you find yourself standing at the bar ordering a whiskey or asking your friend for "just one cigarette." Sam was a little nervous. We stuck close to him until people started arriving, all the good-looking art patrons with their shiny hair and expensive black coats.

"Here he is, the famous artist." A short girl with a precise black hair cut, bangs, enormous red lips, and a loosely cut forest-green silk suit came out from behind a partition with her arms extended.

"That's Krim," Sam muttered.

Behind her was a square man with intellectual glasses, also wearing a suit, extremely expensive and well-cut, cuffs falling gently on his saddle shoes.

"And Purdoe."

"Ah." I understood. Krim-Purdoe was the name of the gallery.

The room was now filling with admirers. Eileen and I decided to go look around. Just like everyone else I was keeping one eye peeled for art I wanted to collect and the other for men.

30

When we got back Sam was standing in the doorway smoking and talking to a guy with long straight hair and a small beard and mustache.

"This is Jake," he said.

"How do you do?" I said.

Krim (I knew she had to have a more feminine first name but I still hadn't heard it) appeared by Sam's side, gently tugging, "Sam, there's someone I'd like you to meet."

Sam raised his eyebrows at me. Oh, the pain of being an extremely sought-after artist.

When he left no one said anything for a minute. I sure knew Eileen wasn't going to help. I didn't know what the story was with this Jake guy, but I was in a good mood.

"Live in New York?" I asked him.

"Uh huh, yes."

"From here?"

He smiled. "Nope, I'm from Oklahoma."

I could hear it in his voice.

"But you live here now."

"Yep. Where are you from?"

"Well, hmmm. I grew up in California, but I've lived in a lot of places since then. The last one before New York was Albuquerque."

"Oh yeah?" I could hear the interest in his voice. "D'you like it there?"

"Yes. Very much. Yes, I loved it. The conceptual basis of existence is entirely different than in New York. Because the cultural mix is strong, with Hispanic and Indian ideas—dreams, magic, and all this . . ." I spread my arms to take in what was going on at that moment, the art and us talking, the white walls of the hallway, "have fluid boundaries. For example, when you go to Europe, there's history in the land. If you go to the Plaza Major, the place in Madrid where they tortured people during the Inquisition, you can *feel* the blood in the ground—it affects everything. In New Mexico, there's that kind of ancient history, but it's two thousand years of peaceful Anasazi Indian culture."

"Umm, hmmm. What do you do here in New York?"

"Secretary. I'm a secretary."

Out of the corner of my eye I noticed Eileen staring at me.

"And that's all?"

I raised one eyebrow. "I can't concentrate on more than one thing at a time."

Sam came back. "Sorry about that."

Jake looked straight at me. "Sam, what does she do?"

31

Sam was confused at the slight threat in Jake's tone. "Everything, but mostly writes stories. I don't know how to describe them, but they're pretty good."

Jake smiled at me. "I caught you."

I smiled too at the idea of one person in New York "catching" another doing art.

"Listen," Sam said to Jake. "We're going to dinner soon. If you want to join us, you're more than welcome."

"Yeah, I'd like to," Jake said.

"Okay, I'll just let Krim-Purdoe know. They were giving me some trouble earlier about how many people I could invite but I'm sure they won't mind you coming."

"Been here a long time?" Jake asked me.

"Not quite two years. That's what I told myself. I had to stay two years. I almost left many times. For the first three months I even had a plane ticket back."

"Are you sorry you stayed?"

"Yes and no. You know, in one way, I can't be too sorry about even the most horrible things that have happened because it's all gone into making me how I am." I unconsciously pushed my hands down my hips. "But I worry too. Like my ambition is possibly at war with my moral stance."

"Yeah, I think I know what you mean."

We both looked into the gallery and saw Sam talking to Purdoe and Krim while they turned out the lights in the back. Another woman, tall and elegant with a long swinging auburn pageboy, was with them. She was smoking a cigarette in an ivory holder.

Sam came over. "We might as well head on out. David told me where the restaurant is. The corner of Spring and Lafayette." The four of us started toward the elevator.

Eileen finally spoke up. "I think I'm going to go home. Will we pass by a subway I can take?"

All three of us looked at her.

"Sure. I'll show you," I said.

A block later the green light over the station appeared.

"You're welcome to come along," Sam said.

"No, no, I guess I better go home." Eileen seemed even more on edge than usual.

"Okay."

"You can change for the express at 14th Street," I told her. "Do you have enough money?"

"Yeah, I'm okay." She disappeared underground.

I shrugged at Sam.

"You were right. She is fucked up," he said.

Jake just looked at us.

We walked another block to an Italian restaurant. Sam held the door for me. The interior was dark and decorated with red glass. We were shown to a back room.

Jake sat beside me and Sam sat down next to him.

We looked around.

"I guess we get a private room," Sam said.

"Yeah, but they seem to have deserted us. Do you want me to go out and ask for a bottle of wine?" Jake asked.

Sam swung his head dolorously around. "That's a great idea."

We watched Jake walk to the front.

"You know Jake's a painter, too," Sam said as soon as he left.

The rest of the party arrived. Krim, Purdoe—whose first name I figured out was David—a woman who seemed to be with Krim with the same smooth black hair and big red lips, and the woman with the cigarette holder, who sat down next to Sam.

"Kenny, have you ever met June?" Sam asked her.

"I don't believe I have. I've heard a lot about you, though. Isn't he staying at your apartment here?" she said.

I smiled. Whatever she had heard, bad or good, I was sure it was exaggerated and therefore great publicity.

"Kenny is my dealer in Chicago," Sam said to me.

"Ah, yes, well then, I've heard about you too. Your gallery has a very good reputation."

"Where do you live?" she asked me in a slightly catty way.

"Actually, I'm planning on moving to Harlem, but I kept my place in SoHo so it'd be easy for Sam."

Kenny looked surprised, then recovered. "That's a true friend."

Jake looked at me.

She turned to David Purdoe and asked him if he'd seen Alton, the reviewer for the *Village Voice*.

"No, he was there?"

Jake asked me if I'd like some wine.

"No thank you, but if you'd help me clear a place in front of us so the waiter who's bringing the appetizers will put them down here, I'd be very happy."

"I'd like that, too." He took the centerpiece of artificial flowers and put them on a table behind me. Just then the red-coated waiter arrived bearing a silver tray with antipasti—salami, mozzarella, prosciutto, pickled vegetables, radishes, and cheese puff pastries piping hot.

"I'm hungry," I said.

"Me too."

We both filled our little plates with Italian appetizers.

"I want some of those peppers," I said.

He reached to get me some. There was definitely a buzz between us.

Kenny looked down at us and arched her eyebrow ever so slightly. "How're things with your wife, Jake?"

Sam smiled at no one.

Jake frowned, also at no one. "Better. A little better. We're seeing a marriage counselor. It seems like things are working out, at least so we can tolerate each other."

"Well, I remember you were having serious problems the last time I talked to you on the phone. I think that was right before the big show at the Los Angeles County Museum, right? How'd that show go?"

"Good, it was pretty good."

"Sam told me you sold out."

"Yeah," Jake mumbled into his plate.

I was looking at him while I ate a flaky pastry filled with spinach and ricotta cheese. He was kind of cute. It was too bad he had that beard and mustache. And a wife. And he drank. Well, it didn't matter anyway.

The Day After We Go to Jake's Studio Downtown

"Hi." A woman with a small pointy face and short light brown hair, blue jeans, and a baggy white sweater—not enough clothing for the weather, I thought—smiled at us. The three of us were all headed for the service elevator.

Sam clanged shut the iron door then the inner steel lattice door and we went up.

The woman got out on the second floor with us.

"Jake's?" she asked with an accent, sort of German-sounding.

"Yeah."

She walked across a hall, opened the green door, and ushered us in. The room was rectangular, about forty feet by twenty feet, with dark green walls.

The ceilings were high, fifteen feet high. Near the top edge of the wall opposite the door was a skylight. Around the edges of the room were paintings leaning against the walls. Landscapes with green hills and white flat skies, shells, small mountains. Some with ducks. Smokestacks with writing on them. Most of the paintings had small rural backgrounds and a single large, almost central object.

They were great. Looking at them reminded me of the flashes I get sometimes walking on an overpass and suddenly seeing an expanse of huge clouded sky, or looking down Fifth Avenue and changing my focus to ALL THE WAY down the street and realizing that I am free now, no longer subject to the whims of grown-ups. I walked back and forth in front of the paintings and didn't say a word. The sexual thing with Jake got much stronger, the air between us became solid: I felt that if I moved toward him the air would push against him. It was as if he was brushing his fingertips along the edge of my stomach. I knew what the softness of his lips would feel like.

"You have two shows coming up, don't you?" Sam asked.

"Yeah. One here, one in Finland."

"Finland?" Sam sounded impressed. "That'll be good for you, won't it?"

Jake smiled just a little. "Maybe."

His assistant, the woman with the German-sounding accent, who'd been working unobtrusively all this time, walked over and stood near Jake, waiting for him to finish. He looked at her.

"We need more gesso and tape," she said.

"Do you want to go to the store? The weather is terrible."

"I don't care."

"Okay, get me some cadmium white too, then. Here's the keys to the car. It's over on West Broadway."

"I'd rather walk." She smiled and got her coat.

We didn't say anything else before she left. Jake wanted to talk about her and another subject would interfere.

"She's good," Jake said. "It's good for me. She's gay."

"Where's she from?" Sam asked.

"She's Dutch. My last assistant was good, too, but . . ." He let the rest of the sentence go and walked over and picked up a thick sketchbook. "Look at these."

Sam went over and started looking through the book. I didn't know if I was invited, but after a minute I walked over too. There were sketches of bleak land, some abstracts, his name in watercolors written like Chinese letters down the page, and then women. Women as cartoon characters, cheesecake and Vargas girls, but better, with more dimensions to their character. Sam was looking at them avidly.

"Can I have one of these?" He asked.

Jake shrugged. "Take your pick."

Sam turned the pages back and forth, excited that he was going to get one of the women.

"My last assistant"—Jake looked right at me—"left because we started having an affair. For a long time, working together was fine. She was a hard worker. It was a year before anything happened. Then I knew we started to be attracted to each other. When she would bring me a brush I would get turned on. And one day she said, 'Come here.' I went over and she started kissing me. For about a week it was fine. It lasted longer than that of course, but stuff got all fucked up. How could she be my lover and my assistant too, you know? I didn't think it was cool anymore to tell her to clean the bathroom."

Sam was turning the pages. Pictures of women, white sky, silos, wheat fields.

"But you like having female assistants?" I asked.

"Yes."

"How come?"

"They can do two things at once. They can clean the desk and order paint on the telephone. They are more organized."

"I don't think that's true," Sam said in his slow drawl. "Men are more organized."

Jake shrugged his shoulders. "Do you want to get out of here soon? When Becky gets back I'll be about ready for a beer."

"Great idea," Sam said.

I went to the other side of the room and paced back and forth in front of the paintings. They were so great. I felt lightheaded being there. The lone mallard soaring across the sky—I thought, of course that's what he would paint now that he was successful, flying. And he was so completely sure.

Becky came back and we all left together.

She said good-bye outside and went off toward the subway. It was still snowing big fat wet flakes and the sidewalks were piled high with white slush. Jake put a manila envelope inside his heavy brown overcoat.

"Just up the street is this place you'll love, Sam. Talk about leaving New York City."

He steered us toward a dark wood doorway over which glowed a Budweiser sign.

Inside was also dark, the color of old stained log cabins, lit only by a hooded lamp over the pool table and various beer signs. The room was filled with men with deer hunting caps and unshaven faces, plaid shirts buttoned over tight bellies, hair long and straggly. The only woman was playing pool. She had blue jeans tight over the heft of her hips and a white blouse, breasts pushing against the ruffled front, and a cowboy hat. It was obvious from the set of her mouth that she really could play. The light shone on the top of her poised pool cue while she remained motionless, calculating the shot.

We went to a small round table in the dark back of the room. Jake was sitting right next to me while Sam stayed standing and asked what we wanted to drink.

I was acutely aware of the tops of my thighs, my hips. Alert. My legs were sending signals about how the cotton material of my stockings felt, about how much they wanted to be touched by the thick strong painter hands that were even then resting on the table. I looked at him. Round face, eyes with layers of experience. Sexy, lanky straight hair.

"What'd you think of the studio?"

"I loved it."

"I'm sorry about my wife. We married too young. I love my kids, that's why I'm going to therapy with her. I went fishing with my little boy last weekend. He caught a fish that was too big for him to hold onto." He smiled. "I watched him let it go and then we talked about what it was like to try to make a living." He looked down at his hands on the table. "I think if two people are going to have a thing, it's the woman who decides it, don't you agree?"

"Yes." I was having an incredibly difficult time not touching him.

"What are you going to do for the next six months?"

"Go to school. I'm going to Columbia. I just started. And working."

"You'll be pretty busy, hunh?"

"I hope not too busy."

"Okay, whatever you say."

Sam returned with two beers and a soda.

Helen Calls

"June?"

"Helen!"

"I got your message. I miss you."

"I know. I feel like I've moved to another town. This school thing." I sighed. "It's only for another couple of months. Sorry I didn't call sooner."

37

"Heard that before. But not usually from a sister."

My own sudden wild laugh surprised me. "Isn't that true. Yeah, men, their time thing is all fucked up."

"Do you think that's what it is?" Helen said without the slightest hint of sarcasm in her voice.

"Of course. One problem is that time is different for a man than for a woman. You know that when you like some guy you can think about him all day long. The whole time you are working you think about him, too. You just split the screen. One part of your mind thinks about work, the other about your love object." I laughed.

"You mean men don't do that? But I've had men say to me that they can't get me out of their mind."

"Yes, sometimes. But I bet they don't get any work done either. Men have been trained in this different way, and when they are thinking about work, they are not thinking about you. So if a day and a half goes by you can think about them one million times but they have only thought of you ten times, and then when you see them it seems as though a lot more time has elapsed since you actually saw them in person."

"Oh, yeah, Andrew knows about women's ability to split the screen, he brings it up whenever he sees me doing a layout and talking on the telephone. He says he's seen women talk on the telephone and add a column of numbers."

"I was having this conversation with this painter guy last week and he said he always hires women assistants because they are better workers. And that's exactly it. Because they know how to split the screen."

I Deliver the Computer to Julianna, My Editor

The phone rang.

"Pardon me," Julianna said and got up from the table to answer it.

Alison, Felix and I kept talking. Felix and Alison were a great couple. Felix had his hair cut short like a criminal, it reminded me of Wilbur. He had the same kind of really sexy Eastern European round head too. Alison's strawberry blonde hair stuck up in many different directions, which along with her pert nose gave her a pixie-ish look despite her height.

"I'm not that crazy about David Lynch," Alison said, frowning only with her eyebrows. "It just seems to me he does weird stuff for its own sake. You know, I'm like anyone else. I love weird stuff if there's a reason for it, or if it suddenly pops out even though a great deal of effort has gone into suppressing it, but I always feel with him that he's just throwing things in to shock an audience he doesn't think of as composed of his peers, but as little mean librarians and big-assed nasty office managers. But I don't know, maybe I'm stupid. A lot of my good friends love him."

Felix and I laughed.

I said, "I agree with you, but usually keep my opinion to myself. *Eraserhead*, though, I have to say, was genuinely disturbing."

"I never saw it," Alison said.

"Yeah, well, I don't know if I'd say I *recommend* it. I mean, it still sometimes enters my mind and gives me the creeps when I'm about to have a horrible nightmare or have just had one, so it is—oh, I'll say it is pretty powerful."

"Yeah, it's like walking in on your least favorite uncle's suicide," Felix said. "Okay, you're an adult, you didn't like him that much anyway so you should be able to get over it, but chances are good the image is never going to fade. Now John Waters is a different story," he said. "There's a man who is genuinely weird."

"Oh, I love him," Alison said.

"Me too. Have you ever read any interviews with him?" I asked. "I always want him to be my friend."

Julianna hung up the telephone. "Sorry about that."

Julianna was wearing a smocked dress with dark blue triangles intermittently printed on it over black velvet leggings. Her thick auburn hair fell straight to the middle of her back where it was blunt cut. Her hair had so much weight and volume that it seemed fuller at the bottom than the top.

"He's still in St. Louis?" Alison asked.

"Yeah, yeah. He's having a miserable time. Flat on his back every night. He told me he's in incredible pain and can barely move."

I looked at her politely, thinking she was talking about her boyfriend, but not wanting to seem nosy when she'd been so secretive about him at work. We were distracted for a minute by Alison and Felix leaving.

"How's he like St. Louis?"

"He hates it. He says there's nothing to do unless you want to drive around and look at the white people reclaiming old Southern buildings and that every single person has one of those giant plastic cups with a straw coming out of it welded to their hands. I don't know what he's talking about, he says they get them at 7-11 or something."

I laughed. "That's great. That's the greatest thing because you know, my mother is from St. Louis, and even though she lives in California, *she* always has one of those giant plastic cups. No one else in the family ever does. She even takes it in to see her therapist."

"Wait until I tell him. He'll love that. I thought he was just exaggerating."

"No, no. It must be something. You know that city has a strange, special culture, not like any other city. Decayed old South like New Orleans, but with this hopeless nostalgia for when they actually were some kind of industrial power, maybe a hundred years ago, because at that time everyone had to go through there to get West. I'm sure the plastic cups have a connection with that."

"Oh, this is exactly the kind of stuff he loves." Then her face got serious. "Do you know who I'm talking about?"

I was surprised. Maybe I'd gone too far in my assumption. Maybe she didn't want me to know, and I'd now seemed like I'd been prying by figuring it out. "Oh, sorry, I thought it was your boyfriend you told me about that day at work."

"You know?"

"Oh, yeah, well, you told me sort of, at least the fact that you were having an affair with one of the authors and you asked me if I knew which one. Don't you remember this? And I said it seemed like you got a lot of phone calls from Hank Richardson."

She relaxed. "Yeah, that's right."

"Well, he must feel pretty strongly about you because he sure does call a lot."

She looked at me seriously, which was kind of like how she looked at you anyway. "It's really fucked up. You know, don't you, that he's married? He's been married for twenty years."

"Yeah, I thought there was something like that."

"And he lives in Vermont."

"That's bad."

"My therapist says I have to get out of the habit of thinking that that's all I deserve. But I'm reluctant to give it up because I didn't go out with anyone for five years before that." She snuck a look out from under her heavy eyelashes.

"Did you meet him at work?"

"Of course. I was editing his politics of art book. I talked to him a little before then, because you know he published his book of essays—hmmm, did I give you that book on the change in art criticism—right before I started working there. He would call a lot. He'd already figured out that Sol is an idiot and so he asked to talk to me. But it wasn't until I edited his book that I started to get to know him."

"That's proof you're a great editor, because no writer would have an affair with an editor unless they were pretty close to perfect."

She looked a little surprised. Not too much—Julianna was not a person whose feelings showed on her face. "I never thought of it that way. Do you really think so?"

I laughed. "I know for sure."

"You know, I had heard of him a long time before I met him. I went to college in Massachusetts, a small town in the north part of the state and there was only one store that sold *Critique*. My friend Stanley, who was the most enormous and completely insane black guy and Doris, who was kind of a hippie, and I would go down there on Thursday afternoons and wait for *Critique* and I always said the only good writer in it was Hank Richardson. So we would wait in this small bookstore, they had a little café in the middle, and the three of us would divide the magazine. I always got his column to read first."

"He knows this?"

"Oh yeah. I tell him everything."

"I don't know. It seems like he's pretty nice to you, at least."

"Except for the fact that he's married and there certainly isn't any chance he's going to get a divorce. You know, this is a pattern for him, he has affairs with women he meets through his work. They last anywhere from a year and a half to eight years."

"How long have you been seeing him?"

"Just about a year and a half. Pretty depressing, huh?"

"I'm not sure. How does it make you feel?"

"When I'm with him I feel great, and for a little while afterwards. Of course I go through all the fantasies that this time he'll realize and he will divorce his wife. He does say that he's closer to me than any of the other people he's ever had an affair with. But I don't know, people like to hear that. Maybe he believes it, but it might not be true."

"No, I would believe him. I think it's probably true. First of all, men, unless they're real hustlers, don't lie about that sort of thing and he doesn't sound like a hustler to me. And secondly, I see you and I can see that you are a great woman. You have that thing of being extremely sexy that not everyone has and you're also smart, thoughtful, and funny. And honest. It's not that many women who have all those things in combination." I was serious.

"Why June, thank you, how nice of you to say so."

"Well, okay, it's okay." Now I was embarrassed. "Just take that information and apply it when you're thinking about your relationship with him."

"Eventually I'll have to get out of it."

"Yeah, well, whenever people start talking about how they don't know whether the relationship will last forever I tell them to forget it. It's much better to have a relationship with someone *assuming* that it's only going to last two weeks, and then if it lasts longer, great, another two weeks is great."

"So you don't think this affair is bad?"

"What? Fuck no, here you are, having an affair with one of your idols. I mean how many people ever get to do that? How many teenagers in Keokuk, Iowa do you think actually get to have an affair with Tom Cruise? But that's what you're doing. And it sounds to me like he loves you too, like this is a serious thing for him. And he respects you as an editor. So, big deal, he's married. I guess she knows he has affairs. And big deal that it won't last forever. Just don't worry about that now when it's still going on. It seems like it's okay to me, the only problem is, you know, the thing of you always torturing yourself about it. That's probably not so great. If someone comes along, younger, unattached, but just as smart and stimulating, then fuck it, you can run off with him, but for now you might as well enjoy what you have."

"You really think so?" She looked skeptical but hopeful. "Maybe."

I laughed.

She looked around. "You said you had somewhere to go? I better call a car service for you."

"Yeah, okay."

I looked at her books while she called.

"You know, I don't know why I said I'd meet these people," I said. "Another date. I hate fucking dates, what's the point of them? I meet these guys and in the long run I never end up liking them. You know, that's another thing. Sometimes I meet guys and they are completely beautiful or charming or something and I get a big thing for them but the more I know them the more my desire for them fades until finally it's gone. What I should start doing is, if I meet someone I like, just fuck them right away before I have a chance to find out what they're like."

"Let's go in the front room," she said. "So we don't miss your car."

42

Djordje

i tre merli **is a very chic restaurant in SoHo with high brick walls and a long mahogany bar.** Small white-linen-covered tables filled with Italian girls in $1500 see-through shirts. Once I'd read an article that said it was a hangout for Young Turks. I wondered, what did they mean when they said Young Turks? Up and comers? Probably so, but whenever I went there everyone was extremely handsome and dark-skinned.

So Wednesday night I had taken my friend Lana to meet my roommate Antonio. What the hell, I thought, he needed a girlfriend and she loved Italian men and my feelings about both of them were similar, so maybe they'd get along. He was about to become a famous film director—she would like that—and they were both tall. The problem was that the next night she wanted to introduce me to a friend of hers, Chuck. I wasn't that interested. She said he had blond hair and blue eyes, which I don't like, and then later it slipped out that he drank too much, and I definitely don't want more of that.

But she begged me, so I agreed to meet her at *i tre merli* at ten o'clock. She told me she and Chuck drank there every Thursday night.

Things, like they so often did in New York, got out of control. I had to take my computer to Brooklyn and I thought I'd be there at seven-thirty and instead at nine o'clock I was in a traffic jam on the Williamsburg Bridge, doing breathing exercises to not freak out. When I got to my editor Julianna's house she had made dinner and was waiting for me with her roommate Alison and Alison's boyfriend Felix. I wasn't even hungry but after being that late I could hardly stay for only ten minutes. I figured that if Lana and Chuck went to *i tre merli* every Thursday, what difference did it make if I was there right away or not?

I arrived at eleven. Rushing through the crowd in my black miniskirt, high heels, and huge purple plastic purse, I happened to notice that the place was jam-packed with the most gorgeous, exquisitely dressed, perfectly muscled men. Lana sure knew what she was doing, I thought.

Finally I spotted her. She was sad and a little tipsy. Chuck was gone.

"He said no woman keeps him waiting an hour."

"Okay," I said, truly relieved not to have to talk to any men. "I mostly came to see you anyway."

She brightened. "Does that mean you'll hang out with me for the rest of the night?"

"Sure," I said, then remembered, looked at my watch. "Uh, no, I take that back. I can only hang out with you for twenty minutes. I have to go home and make some calls. Business calls."

43

Sort of business, trying to fix some fights I was having with an ex-girlfriend of my brother's. She worked at a magazine.

"How long can you stay out?" She looked confused.

"About half an hour." I paused, sensing her disappointment. "Okay, maybe a little bit more."

She turned and started talking to a man who looked to me like he was sneering. I had an idea that he had been stalking her.

After a second he left and she turned back to me.

"So what do you want to do? Do you want to go to *Jour et Nuit?*"

"Sure, okay."

"Or do you want to stay here?"

"Whatever you want."

"Chuck said he was going to *Jour et Nuit* so maybe we could find him. I really wanted him to meet you."

"All right," I said, though actually I wasn't wild about the renewed possibility of meeting him.

"Okay. We'll go down there, if that's okay with you."

"Of course." And quick as a wink I was through the crowd, out the door, and on the sidewalk, looking once again at my watch. I was pacing back and forth. I looked back in—the front of *i tre merli* is made of french doors that fold back completely, so it was open to the warm spring night. I could see back through the smoky high-ceilinged room, but Lana wasn't coming.

I walked back and forth impatiently.

Finally she appeared.

"June? Listen, do you want to go to the opening of a new club? Because there are two guys in there who invited us to go to a club."

"That sounds interesting." The last thing I wanted to do was go to the opening of a club. A million nights in my life I would have given my right arm to go but not tonight.

"Okay. I have an idea." She looked at me apologetically, but clearly excited. "How about you stay here with the guys and I'll go to *Jour et Nuit* and see if I can find Chuck?"

"Okay."

"You will?" She seemed totally surprised. Was it that she thought I would object to the morality of trying to corral as many men as possible, or was she accustomed to girlfriends who couldn't be left alone for even a second?

But she wasn't going to test her luck. She turned to lead me back into *i tre merli.*

I saw the guys before we got to them. They were tall and very handsome, one with dark hair and bedroom eyes, the same guy I thought might have been sneering earlier, and one with lots of straight sandy hair. I was thinking they weren't going to be too happy with the substitution of serious small me with my eyebrow raised speculatively over my sunglasses ("So you're in mergers and acquisitions? Have you any moral qualms about that?") for the lovely tall slightly drunk flirtatious Lana.

She performed the introductions and we began a conversation.

"What do you do?" asked the dark one, whose name I heard as George. Could that really be? He had some kind of Eastern European accent; people there didn't name their sons George, did they?

"Write."

"Are you famous?"

I looked at him. "If I were, you would probably already know who I was, right?"

He smiled. "And you wouldn't be talking to me."

I smiled back.

"What kind of things do you write?"

"Strange fiction. Stories."

"Like what? Have you had anything published?"

I was getting nervous being in the spotlight. He sure was a beautiful man.

"Yes. What do you do?"

"I'm a waiter. I wait tables."

Now I was really impressed. No one in New York ever told you they waited tables. I liked him.

"Oh yeah? Where?"

"It doesn't matter. An Italian restaurant on 53rd. I have an idea, too, about business. I'm trying to sell it to Charivari. It's perfect for that store, but they're cheap. They don't want to pay what the idea is worth."

"What's the idea?"

He looked at me disbelievingly.

"Oh, I'm sorry. I forgot how easily ideas are stolen. That was a stupid question. Can you take the idea to someone else?"

He frowned. "Yes, sort of. But it's so perfect for those stores, I'd like to sell it to them if I could. But never mind, it's so boring to talk about business. Are you related to any movie stars or political figures?"

I laughed. "No. I have a sister who might become one. She lives in Los Angeles."

"Have you ever lived there?" He looked straight into my eyes.

I was wondering where *he* had lived.

Lana came back and I remembered I had only been holding her place. I put my sunglasses on and turned to look at the crowd.

"How was the other place?" he asked her.

"It was pretty good." Then she got more enthusiastic. "Great. It was really great."

"Can I buy you a drink?" he asked both of us, and when she said, "Yes, a rum and orange juice," he turned toward the bar.

She leaned closer to me. "Chuck is down there and he said for me to bring you down, he'd still like to meet you, but he's only going to be there for half an hour."

"Okay," I said.

"Don't you want to go down there?" she asked.

Luckily George turned back around with the drinks at just that moment.

"Do you speak French?" George asked Lana.

"Oui. Oui, j'avais habité à Monte Carlo pour deux ans."

"Oui? C'est très bien. Pourquoi habitais-tu là-bas?"

Just as I was feeling forlorn at losing him, I felt his fingers secretly tap my side, as if to reassure me, it's you I'm interested in. I liked him even better.

His sandy-haired friend came back over.

"Misha, did you meet June?"

Misha bowed deeply and kissed my hand. "So lovely. So beautiful."

I laughed.

Misha continued. "And of course I have been anxiously awaiting the return of the amazing and gorgeous Lana." He bowed, kissing her hand, and murmured something to her. Lana smiled up at him. They began talking.

A rather drunk young man in a tight-fitting pinstriped suit and an unquenchably eager look in his bright eyes walked up to George and me, holding a white gym bag.

"The man who owns this bag makes five hundred thousand dollars a year," he said to us proudly.

"And I hope that's not the reason you're carrying it," George said.

I restrained myself from laughing aloud.

"New York is a very strange place," I said.

"Not very healthy." He looked at me.

I smiled.

"Do you ever leave?" I asked him.

"No, I don't have enough money to leave. Do you leave?"

I paused for a second. "I'm going to New Mexico for the summer."

"When are you going?"

"In about three weeks. The beginning of June. I'm not exactly positive when."

"Why there?"

"New Mexico is a magic place. And also I used to live there, so when I go back all my friends are really excited to see me and they hug me and hug me and kiss me and kiss me and in New York I never get touched." I looked straight at him.

I leaned down and smelled his drink. "Scotch."

"Have some."

"No, thank you."

We noticed that Misha had left rather abruptly. Lana was standing by herself again.

"Your friend is very rude," she said to George.

"Why do you say that?"

"He asked if he could kiss me!" She sounded indignant.

"Oh, he was just joking."

So George was loyal, too.

"No, he wasn't. No man asks a woman to kiss him unless he means it." Lana was even more indignant now.

"Kiss me," George said to her with just enough sincerity that possibly he might mean it, even though all three of us knew perfectly well what would happen if she agreed.

She waved him away with her hand. "Okay. Well, why don't you come with us to *Jour et Nuit*? It'll be fun."

"But I don't want to meet that guy. I don't think I'll like him."

I was excited. George knew what she was doing and possibly didn't want to meet the guy because he knew it was connected with me.

"No," Lana wheedled. "There's no guy down there. Come down. It'll be fun."

"Oh, I don't think so."

"C'mon. You want to go, June, don't you?"

"Well . . ." Definitely, I didn't, for about three different reasons. "Isn't he probably already gone now? Anyway, I have to go practically immediately."

George looked at me. "Don't go. Please don't leave me."

"I have to. Really. I have to."

"Will you write me a letter telling me what you thought of meeting me?"

"Why, yes. That's good. That would be perfect. Absolutely. I would do that."

"I want to hug you and hug you and kiss you and kiss you." And he moved forward ever so gently and kissed me, quick, his tongue violent, then gone.

I was completely in love.

I ran my hands down his sides and noticed the shape of his jacket and the way the pockets were cut into the sides. And the material—silk wool in the subtlest dark gray. He was cool.

"Nice coat."

He raised one eyebrow.

After a minute I looked at my watch again. "I really have to go. Really. I have to go, like, ten minutes ago."

"Please don't."

"Let me go."

"But I don't want you to leave."

"I have to. I swear I'll write."

"Okay then." He released me.

I swung toward Lana and she was talking to a tall, too tall man with WHITE hair in a crewcut, insane BLUE eyes, and a *completely* RED face—I hoped for his sake from the sun, and not from too much alcohol.

"June, this is Chuck."

Oh my god, what was I going to do? I'd already stood the guy up twice before I'd even met him.

I smiled and began talking very fast. "Look, Chuck, I'm really happy to meet you and I know you must be mad, this wasn't very nice of me, but I was stuck in a traffic jam on the Williamsburg Bridge while delivering my computer and I couldn't exactly call you here and then I didn't want to go to *Jour et Nuit* because to tell you the absolute truth"—I looked at my watch again—"I have more business to do tonight and I know you'll be even more pissed and I'm sorry but I really have to leave right this very minute." Then I turned and ran out the door, hailed a cab, said, "354 West 110th," went to finish closing the door and was stopped by George, who got in and said "235 East 35th."

The door closed and we started to move off. I leaned forward, close to the driver. "We'll take him home first, but I still want to go to 354 West 110th. But in the meantime . . ." I swung my leg over and sat on his lap, facing him, "— we can . . ."

After a few minutes I pulled away. "You know, I'm not like this. This is not something I usually do."

"Of course not." George smiled. "No one ever does. But I've seen it on TV and in the movies."

We kissed more. I could feel his whole body pressed against mine. I was wildly excited by his hard-on.

"I'll tell you what," I said. "If you come up to my house and wait in the cab while I make a phone call, I'll come to your house."

"All right," he said in this great way. Not over-eager, like he'd do anything for me, and not resigned, like some men who just think all women are crazy, but just okay, like the same way I would feel, and mean it, as if he were saying, "It's unplanned, but it's okay with me."

We took the long way back from my house, through Central Park. The trees slid by the window. When we got out he paid, then took my hand and pointed ahead to a large brick building with about twenty-three stories. "That's my building. Do you like it?"

Upstairs I wandered around the large studio with white carpeting. A man's house—not much furniture, not much use of the kitchen. Only the slightest smell of cigarettes; he must smoke mainly when he's out.

I walked back and forth—no, I *strutted* in my short skirt, teasing him.

"I have to call my aunt," he said.

"I have to go to the bathroom."

He pushed the door open with his foot. He already was dialing the phone, his foot in front of the door, making it impossible for me to even think of closing it. I wondered if this was on purpose—must be, he seemed to be always thinking. So, a test.

He got off the phone while I was still peeing, walked over, and pulled out his cock. I love to suck cock. I wonder if it's weird and anti-feminist of me. I think about sucking cock sometimes when I'm walking down the street—like, I'm on my way to the bank, should I be ashamed, should I be worried someone will find out? Would my girlfriends be disgusted? I'm in heaven, he's beautiful.

We went over to the bed and lay there kissing again.

He said, "Would you mind washing your hands?"

For the first time I was shocked. "No, sure. Whatever." I went and did it.

"It's just the city. I watched you. You touch everything. The glasses, your friend . . ."

I didn't say anything. He washed his hands too.

I went back to the bed and took off my dress. As always, I had on black underwear. I like the way it looks against my white skin. I got on all fours and watched him.

"You are incredibly beautiful," he said.

He came over. He put a rubber on, looking straight into my eyes while he did it, almost accusatorily, or proud—something. I just liked it that we didn't have to have a discussion; he just did it. That was cool. It felt great, I was so turned on already. He was big—big cock, big body, smooth man muscles.

49

He started slow then went faster. I gripped him with my thighs to make him slow down again.

He was talking in my ear. "I want to make you come. I want to make you feel good. Please. I'll come after. I love your body."

I was going crazy.

The phone rang and he answered it, but went right on fucking me. I could see the little beads of sweat on his forehead. "Yes, yes, yes." He smiled at me. "Yes. No. No, I haven't been running." He was looking at me the whole time. "I just got in," he said. "Good-bye." He hung up.

Teasing him, I pulled away and turned over.

"Oh, that's what you want."

"No, no, I was just teasing you. You're too big."

Still, he got up and went to the bathroom and greased his cock.

He came back and lay down behind me and put his hands on my nipples. I was immediately excited, puffed up pussy lips, red hot messages shooting wildly back and forth, brain completely fucking gone.

He pressed his cock against my butt.

"No, no."

"Oh yeah, please. You'll be so tight."

"No, you're too big."

He pushed gently. I rubbed myself. He pushed harder. It hurt, then it felt good. I was losing control.

He was stroking my breasts and muttering in my ear again. I started coming like crazy.

"Can I come in your face?"

"Yeah." More dirty stuff.

He pulled the condom off and I gave him a blow job. The phone rang again. He started coming.

After five rings he answered it.

"Yes. What? No. I just came, that's all."

I was really turned on still. I felt the white chenille bedspread against my skin.

He got off the phone, and pointed to a framed picture on his bedstand.

"My grandmother. My favorite, she's still in Yugoslavia."

"Did you move straight to New York?"

"No, I was in France for a few years. I worked for an airline. A woman, a very beautiful woman from the richest family in Switzerland, fell in love with me. We were going to be married, but her family objected. She still would have done it, but I didn't want to live that way, caring terribly about people looking down their noses at me."

He walked over to the kitchen, lit a cigarette and smiled at me.

"I'm going to take a shower," he said.

"Okay, can I take one with you?"

"Yes, oh yes."

In the Shower With Djordje

I got into the glass-enclosed bathtub with him and he started soaping me, tweaking my nipples.

I loved it, but wondered—was this another cleanliness thing, like making me wash my hands?

"I like you. I like you," he said. "I don't know why."

I smiled.

"That's enough for me." He got out of the shower.

I stayed in; I always forgot how much I love the feeling of warm water on my skin and hair.

He talked loudly so I could hear while he rubbed himself briskly with the white towel. "Do you want kids?"

I turned the shower off and opened the sliding glass door. "Yes. Maybe. It's difficult. I would love to have one baby or maybe two, I don't know. You know, I'm getting old for too many. And the thing of writing. A long time ago I had to think about it seriously and I decided I didn't want to have a baby without a man who would hang around. And he would have to do a major amount of the work. Being a writer comes first." I shrugged my shoulders. "I can tell you this. I never want to get married."

He frowned. "I do. I want to get married and I want to have six or seven children."

I was surprised. Maybe it was because he was Yugoslavian that he hadn't been harangued by former girlfriends who'd watched their mothers be destroyed by having that many children. Maybe it was only in prosperous countries that all the children survived and the fathers worked all the time, so the mothers went insane from being virtually deserted and having an overwhelming amount of work.

"Never," I said.

For a minute he looked distracted. He seemed to make an effort to pull his attention back to the room. "Why not get married?"

I'd thought maybe he was going to ignore my remark.

"Because in marriage—well, at least in this culture, in the United States, when the woman gets married, she becomes second to the man, and I don't want that. I would have children with someone and even possibly be their mate forever, but I wouldn't get married." I wanted to explain this idea better. "You know. I don't mean that I would be *forced* from the outside to be second. I mean *inside*, it's *inside* me. I would put myself second because I grew up in the United States and I wouldn't be able to help myself."

"I don't believe that," he said.

"Well, anyway, I'm afraid." I shrugged my shoulders, hoping we weren't going to argue. He walked back over to the bed and sat down. "Come over here." He patted the bed beside him. "I don't want you to leave."

Yes Yes No

All of a sudden a thought popped into my head. "Do you want me to go home?"

He smiled and walked over to where I was standing with a towel wrapped around me. "I do and don't. I have a girlfriend."

"Oh, oh. Yes. Oh. Of course, I'll go then." I started to go over to get my clothes. He pushed me back on the bed softly.

"Don't leave me yet."

I sighed.

"I'm sad about this." He said. "I don't know what I was doing. Maybe it was because I wasn't smoking pot. Sometimes I go out with Misha and his friends but I never am interested in the women. Usually I smoke, though. I don't know. I was trying to be faithful."

"Maybe it was me. This isn't the first time."

"What?" he said.

"Never mind." How embarrassing it would be to repeat so conceited a remark.

He seemed to forget anyway. "I've been faithful to my girlfriend for over a year and a half. I was hoping this was it. But lately it seems different. Just a little while ago I considered it might be a good idea. We could get married."

"How old is she?"

"Twenty-seven."

"American?"

"Yeah, she's a blonde."

A very lovely one, I imagined.

"Somehow, though, things have been falling apart."

I felt sad. I knew this part. You have to go forward or break up and it's starting to look like you're going to break up and you don't want to do it, you're still so close to the excitement of thinking you finally found someone.

"I have to go," I said.

"Don't."

"But it's late and you should get some sleep." He didn't notice my implication that I didn't need any.

"All right, I'll walk you down. Will you still send me the letter?"

"Yes."

"Can I have your phone number?"

"I don't think so."

"Please."

"I'll think about it and maybe I'll send it with the story."

When he opened the closet door I couldn't help but notice it was filled with jackets, each more perfect than the last. The jeans he wore, too; they were good, the way they molded to his body.

We got in the elevator. He touched me. "I like you. I just like how you are."

"Yeah, I like you too."

He walked me to Third Avenue, going uptown. I hailed a cab and he waved it to go on.

"I like you. I like you," he murmured, burying his face in my neck, then kissing me again and again.

I laughed, kissed him, then turned and hailed another cab.

I kissed him one last time.

"Don't be mad at me," he said sadly as I got in and waved good-bye to him from behind glass.

The next morning, sunny, I woke up jubilant and in tears. I was going on the train that night to Vermont.

All night long, while traveling, in the smallest seat right next to the bathroom and garbage, I wrote him the story, seventeen pages. It got crumpled and then the next week I edited it and crossed out words. The paper I used was scratch paper, on the back was other writing—from my jobs, leftover pieces of legal briefs, computer printouts of other stories, a religion term paper, and a porno detective novel I had written.

Wednesday I went to Helen's house and she dyed my hair purple. As she was working I read the story out loud to her. I couldn't hold the pages, so after I'd read each one I dropped it on the floor and some got blotched with dye. I stepped on a couple of other pages accidentally. I edited it again. Helen told me the last two lines were too romantic so I crossed them out completely.

A week later I sent him the whole dirty piece. No phone number. No return address.

To Go Back, Helen Dyes My Hair

"Hi, Helen, did you get the dye?" I was typing hurriedly as I spoke into the phone.

"What? No. I thought you were getting it."

"Damn. I was a little afraid of that."

"Well, there's nothing we can do now. Why don't you come over anyway?"

"Yeah, all right." I tried to keep myself from being disappointed. I had wanted this so badly for over five days and usually, with my hair, three hours was about as long as I could wait.

I decide to get off the subway at 14th Street and walk down to her house to try to make myself feel better. Anyway, there existed the admittedly slim possibility that at eight at night I might walk past a hairdressing salon that could conceivably have the exact three colors I needed. Yeah, sure.

I was kind of scuffling my feet as I walked down the street.

I tried one beauty salon, but it was closed. I kept going, walking now more quickly between the beggars, models, and punk children. Flashed images assaulted me—rolled blue jeans, braided hair, tie-dye, bruises, red shoes. Oh well, I thought, it wasn't the end of the world, just an excuse to see Helen again tomorrow.

I saw another beauty parlor. A guy was in there by himself. He was counting money, almost ready to close. I scooted in the doorway.

"Do you, by some wild chance, have any of the *Torrids?*"

Without saying anything he reached under the counter and brought out a card with all the colors displayed. "I think I have all of them."

"Oh my god, this is so wonderful." I looked at the card. "Okay. okay." I was really excited. "I need Bodacious Burgundy, Outrageous Cherry, and Salacious Red."

He brought them out. "That'll be $13.69."

I frantically looked through my purse. I held out my money. "I only have thirteen-fifty."

"Look at that money again," he said.

Right. I was trying to give him two tens and three ones.

"Oh, thank you."

I ran the rest of the way to Helen's and called her name outside her door.

She opened the door.

"I got it. I got the hair dye. I found it in a little place when I was walking down the street."

"Wow," Helen said. "If that's not divine beneficence, I don't know what is."

We went inside. I washed her dishes and complained about work.

She said, "Last night, Derwood told me the most brilliant thing. Stupid people are always right."

I looked at her. "Is Darryl your boyfriend?"

She blanched. "He would be horrified to hear someone use that word."

I quickly changed the subject. "I saw this guy today in Saks Fifth Avenue and he looked exactly like he was about to ride to the hounds . . ." Luckily I paused for one second. I was about to finish, "as if there are any fields within a hundred miles of Saks." But Helen chimed in.

"Oh yeah, that look is so brilliant. Darryl does a perfect rider. I can't seem to get close, though I do sometimes wear my lady golfer to work. They don't know what to think."

"We used to ride," I said, partly to cover up my embarrassment at my near miss. "I wanted a horse, like all eight-year-old girls, and my parents were foolish enough to give us one. Then we had riding lessons every Saturday morning and we would try to get out of them so we could watch cartoons. 'You go,' we would urge each other."

Helen laughed. "Are you ready?"

"Yes. I could read you the letter to Djordje."

"Wait a minute, the guy is Yugoslavian and his name is George?"

"I called the phone company and they told me, D..J..O..R..D..J..E."

She laughed.

"The story?"

"Wait until I actually start doing your hair."

"All right."

A couple of minutes later she called to me from the bathroom.

"Hey, June, come in here."

Helen's bathroom had a black and white tile floor, a big bathtub with a transparent green shower curtain, and lots of makeup in baskets. A wooden shelf near the tub held many expensive beauty products.

She had set a stool in the middle of the floor facing the mirror. I could see from my breasts up.

Helen started putting Vaseline on my ears and all around my hairline. It felt great to have her touch me.

I said, "Once my roommate and friend Lucy read me part of an article in *National Geographic* about a tribe that spent every night after dinner picking ticks, lice, and sticks out of each other's hair. Evidently they were a remarkably happy people, so Lucy decided that every night I should look for gray hairs in her head and gently pull them out and she would do the same for me." I looked in the mirror at Helen working on me. "It did feel great."

Helen put a towel on my shoulders.

"As you can see, I'm down to my last towel," she said. She turned the stool so I could see the logo across the towel on my back. Reflected in the mirror was the giant black stencil of the Playboy bunny.

"Wow, Helen, where'd you get this?"

She shrugged, "You know, I used to work there."

"As what?"

She laughed. "The same thing I do now."

"I wanted to be a Playboy bunny when I was young," I said.

"I think I did too."

"How'd you get over it?"

"Working that job, I guess. The way the girls were thought of and treated. Like they were product. We could go to the Playboy Club whenever we wanted, but I could only stand it twice. The way the men treated those girls. No one ever seemed to notice or care that they were actually in pain from their high heels and uniforms. And they were young. Nineteen and twenty years old. How'd you get over the idea?"

"A job where we had to wear very little clothing. A tiny red outfit that ended here." I indicated the very tops of my thighs. "Sort of like Peter Pan. With red underwear and stockings and high heels. At first I thought, 'Oh, good, this is like being a Playboy bunny'—you know, my dream. I thought they would particularly like the fact that I was smart, an intellectual bunny."

"At the job?"

"No, no. In my made-up dream. The job, although at the time I didn't admit it, was a second-rate substitute. The cocktail lounge of the Palmer House, this famous old hotel in Chicago. I worked there for three months. The customers were all conventioneers and they would offer you enormous amounts of money to fuck their clients. It was difficult because you were turning these guys down, but you still wanted them to tip you on their hundred dollar bar tab."

"What'd you say?"

"I said I had very conservative friends and a big mouth. Finally I couldn't stand that job any more. I went out with my boyfriend and Danny—as a matter of fact, the Danny you know—and had three double Southern Comfort Manhattans, and when I went in to work I quit. 'You can't quit,' they said. Do you think anyone has ever paid any attention to that particular remark? I mean, really. Anyway, I walked out."

I began reading the letter to Djordje aloud to her as she applied big globs of wet, dark purple dye to my head. I was using my one hand to hold the towel closed, so when I finished reading a page, I pushed it with my thumb and let it fall to the floor.

It was a little hard to read it to Helen. I didn't know if I knew her well enough. I got to the part about him wanting to have anal sex.

Helen said, "He wanted to have anal sex on the first date?!!"

A little embarrassed, I said, "We did. Here, it's in the story." I kept reading " . . . the phone rang. He answered it. 'Yes. yes, I was just coming, that's all.'"

I looked in the mirror. Helen was watching me with both her rubber-gloved hands in my hair.

She raised her eyebrows at me and drawled, "Would he have told that person he just came if they called while he was beating off?"

When I finished reading the whole thing I asked her, "What'd you think?"

"Take out that last line. It's too romantic. The last two, even. The story is wildly romantic, anyway."

More Djordje

Lana called me. "Misha asked me out."

I was depressed that Djordje would be connected to me in this way, but excited too.

"Do you remember him? He was the friend of that guy you were talking to. Oh yeah, Misha told me you wrote his friend a letter." There was a question in her voice. I had been desperately trying to teach Lana how to play hard to get.

"He asked me to."

"What did you say? How long was it?"

"Seventeen pages."

"Seventeen pages!"

I felt incredibly defensive.

Lana went on. "I did go out with Misha and I like him."

I couldn't help myself. "Did you sleep with him?"

"Yes."

"I thought you yourself said it's not a good idea to sleep with someone on the first date."

"Well, it's not a good idea to sleep with them when you first meet them, foreign men especially, but the first date is okay. It depends on what you want them for."

"Oh, brother."

"I like him, June."

"Who?" My attention had been distracted by a mirror, and besides, Lana had a new crush every other day.

"Misha. He was really nice. And a great lover. Can I call him?"

"No."

"Please," she begged.

"Absolutely not." This was one of my major rules. Do not call men even if you need an ambulance and theirs is the only number you have memorized (which is, unfortunately, highly likely).

"When can I call him?"

"Never."

Misha called her a couple of days later and she called back, got Djordje on the phone. Afterwards she called me.

"I called Misha. I called him back when he called me."

"Okay."

"He's moved. I guess he moved in with George."

Oh no. I was afraid of what was coming.

"George was very nice. He said he would tell Misha I called."

"All right, that's okay. Though in my opinion it's better to hang up if you don't get the guy you wanted to talk to." I was secretly suspicious of my own motives for being so hard-core.

She sounded upset. "How could I tell? They both have Yugoslavian accents!"

"Okay," I relented.

58

"He said for you to call him."

"Maybe."

"You should."

"I'll see how I feel next week. He should call me."

"Jesus, June, he asked for your phone number and you wouldn't give it to him. How do you expect him to call you?"

"He could look it up in the phone book."

"And how many June or J. Smiths do you think there are in the Manhattan directory?"

Actually, I was elated.

"He said you left your watch over there."

"Fuck. Yeah, I did. That was a dumb mistake. I got a new one."

"He asked me. He said, 'She left her watch over here. Do you think it means something?'"

"Tell him to throw it away. No, no, wait. Don't say that. Don't say anything." I was really excited now. I mean I thought this guy was cool. And that was a pretty damn rare event.

"He asked me to come over there."

"What?!" My heart sank. So it *was* any girl.

"He tried to talk me into coming over there. I couldn't, of course. It was the middle of the afternoon. I was at work. Anyway, I should go, but you ought to call him."

No way. I was pissed. And I never did call him.

I'd told Ginka and Helen I'd meet them at the lesbian club, but I just couldn't. I was too tired. The next day I called Helen at her work.

"How was it?"

"To tell you the truth, it was sort of a disappointment, particularly for Ginka. I think she was expecting a glamorous scene, the old-fashioned dykes in plus-fours with their hair slicked back and slim cigars and instead we were the best-dressed people there."

Clare called me late at night. "June?"

"Yes."

"Well, we . . . Wait. How are you?"

"Great. You know, I've been working pretty hard, really, three jobs and school, but I'm surviving it and in a little while I'm going to burst free into some wild partying and dating. A couple more weeks. But what's the story with you? Last I heard you were going to his house, right? You sent me that letter saying you'd called him and he said come over Saturday or something." I took a breath. "There was something else in that letter I was going to ask you about, but I forgot."

"Yeah, well, about Sam—I did go and it was pretty good, but I've been depressed. My back's been acting up. I'm pretty worried."

"What? What is it?"

"Okay, you remember what I told you they said when I got out of the hospital."

Clare had scoliosis and when she was young the method of dealing with this ailment, curvature of the spine, which usually struck children between six and twelve, was to put them in traction for many years. In the case of children whose parents did not have a lot of money—and this was definitely the case with Clare—they were sent to the closest state hospital. Although her family lived in Ohio, Clare had spent six years lying in extremely painful metal traction in a hospital bed in Lexington, Kentucky. Her parents, with five other children to raise, tried to visit as frequently as possible.

When they did come it was usually for only a few hours. Her father would sit by the bedside and hold her hand and talk to her about his life as a carpenter. He would bring her toys carved of wood. Her mother, who always wore sunglasses and a full-length black leather trenchcoat, would gaze out the hospital window.

"So what is it?" I asked.

"I've just been in more pain than usual. So I'm suicidal. That's not the only reason. I'm sure I'll never have a boyfriend again. I went to some gallery openings yesterday and everywhere I looked there were guys, guys that looked kind of interesting, maybe artists or at least they had some kind of idea about art or they wouldn't be there, and it seemed like—I mean, this could just be how I see things through my totally depressed eyes—but it seemed like they were all with these unbelievably young, smooth-skinned blondes."

I laughed. "They probably were. That's how men are. I swear, you have to teach each one individually what fun really is. Have you got a doctor?"

"Yes. He's the top orthopedist in the state, but you know what that means. I have an appointment in three weeks."

"Three weeks?" I was just repeating what she said because I didn't know how to comfort her.

"I'm thinking I should make an appointment with my therapist, too. I slept all day yesterday and when I wasn't sleeping I was crying."

"Oh Clare."

"It kept me out of trouble though. And I did see a great movie on TV. *The Naked Kiss*, do you know it?"

"No."

"Well, it's about this really sleazy man—it's an old movie in black and white. Actually, I'm not going to tell you anything about it because I don't want to ruin it for you. If you ever get a chance to, see it. You could, probably. Do you have a VCR? Never mind, I know the answer to that question. But you probably know someone with a VCR, so get them to rent it and go over to their house."

"Okay."

"All right, I'll be interested to hear what you think because I thought it was great."

"What about going over to Sam's? In your letter it sounded like that went well."

"Yes. It did. Even though, I have to say, his new studio is in a rather daunting area of town. The streets are all burnt out, the glass in the buildings is broken, through the fences you can spot dark gangs of teenagers running. I parked my car in this alley. Sam told me it'd be safe there, but it didn't look all that great to me—there was trash and graffiti and a dead rat near the street. Anyway, it was still light and I figured when I was ready to go he'd walk me back, which he did. He told me it was perfectly okay, but to tell you the truth, I took that with a grain of salt."

"So what'd you guys do?"

"Not much. He showed me his new paintings. He said he hasn't been doing that much since the shows. His house was very cold. At one point I asked him if I could lie on his bed." Her voice got even sharper. "Because of the cold and I was exhausted by my day. We might get more layoffs at work."

"Yeah?"

"It seemed to make him nervous, though. So I asked him, 'Does it make you too uncomfortable that I'm on your bed?' I told him it wasn't sexual and in fact I didn't want to have sex with him."

"You did?"

"Yeah, well, he got flustered and didn't respond. A little while after that I left."

"I'm sorry. It sounds horrible."

"Oh no." Her voice was fake lilting. "It was all right. It was just that I was so tired I would have been unhappy no matter what happened."

"Yeah, I get like that."

"So I guess we better go because this is expensive." Clare sighed.

I wasn't happy to be hanging up without making Clare laugh. "I know. Every month I can't believe they're going to actually *charge me* to talk to my friends and every month, sure enough, they surprise me and do."

Clare laughed.

"Okay. Bye."

Sam Calls Me Late at Night

"June, hi."

"Sam, hi. Smart of you to figure out to call me after midnight."

"Well, I just got in from having dinner with friends. I'm in Manhattan. I'm having lunch with Jake, Jake Hoving, the painter. Tomorrow."

"Yeah, I remember him, we went over to his studio when you were here in January."

Sam's voice was heavy and slow, like always. "Yeah, yeah, I know now, you two had kind of a thing going."

"He turned me on major big time."

"So'd you ever do anything about it?"

"No, no. Listen—I was thinking about this lately. Maybe you could do me a favor and tell him tomorrow something from me when you see him."

"What?"

"You know, I should have just said it at the time, but I'm too much of an idiot. Stupid. I want you to tell him that I really liked him, that I thought he was wonderful and funny and wildly handsome, but I never called him because, well—I couldn't have an affair with him because he was married. You know, not just the moral thing either, but me. For my own sake. I need someone I can see a lot of, particularly after my last thing with Alan—you know, I told you about that, how he really wanted a mistress, someone he saw on Wednesdays and

Saturdays, and with Jake, it'd be worse. I couldn't stand that."

"Okay. I could tell him that."

"Great. Yeah, good, that'd be good. Oh yeah. And tell him that I went to see his show at Gagosian in March and it was wonderful. That I walked down through Central Park, it was sunny and I was listening to some great music on the Walkman, and when I went into the gallery some guy was in the back room, a silver-haired tycoon, buying art, and the paintings were amazing. Really good. And at that moment I was completely happy."

"Okay, sure. He'll like all this, I'm sure."

"Thanks Sam." I was excited now. "So tomorrow you want to meet me for dinner?"

"Tomorrow. Let me think. Tomorrow would be perfect. What time is good?"

"Nine-thirty."

"Nine-thirty? You eat dinner at nine-thirty?"

"Well there's this guy, this crazy guy I have to meet first, so . . . anyway, I promised, and I'm meeting him at eight-thirty. Before that I have to talk to my sister on the telephone and that takes a little while too."

"Okay, nine-thirty's okay."

Rushed Over, New York Madness, Kissed Good-bye Before the Cab Ride by Stan, Kissed Hello After It by Sam

I couldn't wait to ask him about Jake, but I didn't want him to think that was the thing I was most interested in, so I waited.

"Didn't you tell me you were in a wedding? How was that?"

Sam turned his head sideways and frowned, twisting his mouth, then spoke rapidly. "Hated it. I can tell you I was sweating."

I laughed.

Sam grinned back appreciatively.

"I think I did okay though."

"Pretty nice house." I looked around the apartment where he was staying. It was big—wood floors and solid. You could tell it hadn't been renovated; the door frames and window edges were rounded with layers of paint. There was no furniture. "Who lives here?"

"My friends Deb and Andy used to live here—it was their wedding I went to—but they're moving to Seattle after they get back."

"Where'd they go on their honeymoon?"

"Florence."

"Oh, yeah. That's nice. I'd love to go there. But tell me about being the best man."

Sam smiled a tiny bit with his eyes. "I told you it was horrible. I had to do everything. Watch the ring. Get Andy organized. And worse, give speeches. Three of them. Well, I knew about one, at the wedding dinner, so I was prepared. That wasn't too bad once I got here. I'd been tortured trying to write it for three weeks ahead of time in Chicago. But then they sprung those other speeches on me. I had to make something up on the spur of the moment. I was really workin'. You know how I am, June."

"Hey, what's this?"

We were sitting in a living room, which was completely empty except for a yellow-and-green plastic lawn chair that Sam was lying in and an orange director's chair that I had taken. Beside my chair were a couple of pieces of paper that I had just realized were a résumé. I picked them up.

"I'm going to get a beer," Sam said. He hesitated for a second. "Do you want anything? There's not much here. We have water . . ."

"No thank you."

I heard the sound of the refrigerator door shut, hollow in the empty apartment.

I started reading some of his accomplishments out loud. "Corcoran 1986, National Gallery 1987, Minneapolis Museum of Art 1989, Whitney Biennial 1989, L.A. County Museum 1990—jeez, Sam, this is pretty impressive."

"Yeah." He looked at the paper in my hand. "You know, the funny thing is a guy like Jake Hoving would give his right arm for a résumé like that, but because he lives in New York and I live in Chicago, he makes three or four hundred thousand dollars a year and I'm still just getting by."

I didn't say anything yet. Sam lit a cigarette and put the burnt match in an ashtray on the floor.

"It doesn't seem fair. At the same time, I don't want to live in New York. If I moved here—and I could, I lived here before with Sidney—I wouldn't be able to just do my art like I can in Chicago. I'd have to get a job, probably construction, and I'd be scrabbling around looking for a studio, and it wouldn't be as nice as the place I have now—well, you saw Jake's studio, didn't you? And my new place is about four times the size of my old studio. I just don't think it's worth it."

He looked off into space as if he hadn't quite convinced himself.

"How was Jake?"

"We went to the Mapplethorpe show, some of his minor works."

"How'd you like it?"

"It was okay, I guess. I dunno, it was really graphic. I just don't think it was an appropriate show for two heterosexual males to see together."

"What d'you mean?"

"Well, it made me uncomfortable. Maybe if I was with a girl I wouldn't have minded as much. I'm sure it made Jake uncomfortable too."

"It seems like the show was pretty effective if it bothered you."

"I didn't say it bothered me."

"All right. It seems like the show was pretty effective if it made you uncomfortable."

He looked uncomfortable again.

"But did you tell Jake what I said?"

He smiled. Sam knew perfectly well what I wanted.

"Yeah, yeah. I told him the whole thing."

"You told him about how I went to his show and everything?"

"Yeah."

"So what'd he say? How'd he act?"

"He didn't say much, but he smiled a lot when I was talking."

"Did it seem like he liked it?"

"Course he did, June. Who wouldn't like something like that?"

I calmed down. "Okay, thanks Sam. Thanks Sam. Thanks for doing that."

"Maybe you're ready now to go get something to eat," he said.

"What about the thing with Clare?" I asked.

"What about it?"

"Well, you know, we talk, though I haven't talked to her in a long time. I was just wondering what had happened. Did you ever call her again?" I pretended haziness. "Didn't you say you were going to call and then it was a week later or something? I can't remember."

"I meant to call her. I was going to call her, I just forgot for a couple of days and then it seemed like she was going to be mad at me. Then I forgot for more days and I was scared sort of, so I never called her. Why? Are you mad at me about it?"

"I guess I sort of am. You know you should have the guts to do what you say you're going to. You know? Like, there's a million men in the world who do the same things. You know, you slept with her. You should have the balls to tell her you're not going to go out with her."

"But it wasn't exactly that I was attracted to her. I have another girlfriend. I think you know about her. Kim." He laughed nervously and loud. "It was Clare, as a matter of fact, who pointed out to me that I liked her."

My voice was cold. "I think she pointed out to you that Kim was fascinated by you."

"And why shouldn't she be? A big famous artist."

I was completely disgusted. I wanted to say, "You make me sick. A big famous artist known in your own gallery. You believe the hype and you have to get a nineteen-year-old to go out with because she's the only one who believes the hype too." But what good would it do?

We went out to a coffee shop. I only had chicken barley soup.

Lana on the Phone

"Hi, June. It's Lana."
"Can I call you back in ten minutes?"
"Sure."

Inevitably, when I did that, no matter how much I like the person, I didn't want to call them back ever. The pressure of *having* to do things makes me resistant. For example, even for the most fabulous party in the world I always want to decide not to go at the last minute because of the pressure of being expected.

I called her. "Lana?"

"Hi. Did you talk to your roommate Antonio about me?"

"We don't really talk that much. I don't even think I've seen him since Wednesday. Oh, yeah, Thursday, but you already know that. That's when he asked for your phone number."

"He called me. Saturday we're going out."

"So that's good, isn't it?"

"I guess so."

"The man is headed for a giant career as a director. If you want money, this is your golden opportunity." I didn't know why I was acting so hard and mean. I pretended to myself I was kidding.

"We'll see. Misha called me."

I hated this. I was still thinking about Djordje, now it was going to be that thing, two best friends date two best friends, blah, blah, blah. I knew how that always worked out. Everyone broke up.

"Great."

"I'm going out with him on Sunday."

"Ohhh." I dragged the word out. "Full social schedule."

"You know how I hate to stay home."

"Yep. Though then you aren't allowed to complain to me about how you only get hang-ups on your answering machine."

"I hate that."

"Why? I told you: Hang-ups mean someone wants to sleep with you. People should rejoice when they get one."

She laughed.

"Misha was talking again about that letter you sent his roommate."

"I only sent it because he made me promise to write."

"Really?"

"Yeah. Didn't you hear him ask when we were in the bar?"

Lana changed the subject. "Do you think your roommate likes me? Should I go out with him on Saturday? What if Armando calls?"

"I don't think he will."

"What makes you say that?" Her voice got pouty.

"Because you called him too much last week."

"Do you think he'll ever call again?" Now the pout was even more pronounced.

I was stern. "If you don't call him. Your best bet would be to not call him and in about six months run into him when you're with someone you have a far bigger crush on than you ever did on him. Or if you're alone, but cold as ice. Then he won't leave you alone—I guarantee you."

"Maybe I should call him tonight. He's probably been trying to get ahold of me and doesn't want to leave a message on my answering machine."

"He's not."

"How can you be sure? I think Armando's different."

"Go right ahead and believe that if you want, but I'll tell you right now, absolutely there are no exceptions. Never, not one, I have never seen an exception ever. Now, you can pretend like there's a difference because you want for some reason to fuck things up, but I'll tell you right now, that's the rule. You might as well believe that he has x-ray vision. Men don't like women to pursue them."

"That's horrible. Don't we have the same rights as them? That's like saying women don't have any sex drive."

"Yeah, well, when you say it aloud it always sounds bad, but there it is, and if you want to fight it, go ahead, but I'll tell you, the only thing that will happen is your head will get bloody." I emphasized every word. "I think things between men and women have just gotten really fucked up and it used to be you could fool around and break the rules. You remember, you used to just have to ask someone to fuck and they would always say yes, and you could be their girlfriend too, but now it's different. Men are afraid."

"Do you really think so?" Lana asked, but I could tell she didn't believe me anyway.

Thinking About the Movie

Part of why I did the movie was I had a major crush on Helen. Helen is tall and very thin. She's skinnier than a model, but not as smooth—she has too much uncontrolled intelligence in the way she moves her long limbs. She's got straight, shiny brown hair that swings near her chin, deepset eyes and a pointy chin. Helen is headstrong and wild; she grew up in a family with her and four boys. We met through Darryl. On the street.

One day I was over at Helen's. I'd just finished my semester at school and was feeling pretty sporty. Helen was taking pictures of my recently dyed hair. She said, "We should make a movie."

I said, "I would make a movie if I got to have sex with someone I never met before."

So Helen said, "Okay, but you have to tell stories, too."

I agreed to that condition. Later that week I was working as a secretary and the whole script of the movie popped into my head so I typed it up and faxed it to Helen.

She told me to come over to her house Saturday at 10:30. I was pretty excited. One thing I do when I want to look good is go on a fast for three days. So I didn't eat on Thursday and Friday. Since I had to finish moving on Saturday, I got up early and lugged my belongings down five flights of stairs. A roll-up bed, lamp, fan, and some clothes. I tried to get a taxi and the first one wouldn't take me, but the second agreed.

I put on the eleven gold chains I'd bought in New Hampshire the weekend before while shopping with my sister-in-law, a black velvet mini-dress, black stockings (which got a run in them from moving furniture) and black tennis shoes. When I got to her house Helen asked me if I'd like some tea. She was cleaning up a little. Helen has a long brick wall, and in the middle of it a fireplace filled with ritual objects, like carvings, shells, and animals stuffed by the taxidermist.

"We have to go to the store and get batteries for the camera," she said.

"Okay." I figured whatever happened from this point on I'd agree to.

We walked through the hot crowded streets of the East Village, past Tompkins Square Park jam-packed with ragged street people and cardboard homes. We talked. On the way back she made the first mention of the movie.

"It's not going to be sex. I changed it to kissing. I called Andrew and he got too freaked out on the sex idea."

I didn't know why Andrew, her ex-boyfriend, had the final word, but I didn't mind. "Okay. That's okay with me."

"I have some people lined up."

Some people. Well, that would be interesting. A lot different than the one person I had imagined.

"I don't know, anyway, if we're going to be able to get them to do it."

"Yeah, right." I knew it was one thing to propose a wild idea to someone. They always think it sounds great. Often when the actual event came, they backed out.

"We'll just have to set up a structure for them. Not make any mistakes. Like this morning, when I was trying to get a cab to finish my moving and actually I had a little too much stuff for a cab and the first guy I tried to talk into it, I went on explaining for too long. I should have, at one exact point—just started putting my stuff in the car, but I miscalculated and so he drove off. A second cab came and I explained to him and it all went well, he was cool, but that's what I'm talking about. There won't be any second chances."

"Okay," Helen said. "I'll leave that part to you."

"The other thing is to be careful people aren't hurt by this. I don't want anyone to wake up mad four days from now and feel like they've been used."

When we got home Helen said right away, "Hey, c'mere. We're going to do something scary. Grab that candle."

She led me out the door and down the dark hallway through a hidden door. Inside was a stairway. It was musty smelling and there were things crowding the dirty steps leading down, leaving just barely enough room to put your feet. Overhead, revealed by the flickering candlelight, were cobwebs dangling dust. At the bottom was a cement corridor also piled high with ominous forms draped with dirty canvas, then we emerged into a room. I saw, as my eyes readjusted to the light, the kitchen of an apartment. At first it looked dismal, then we kept going into the living room, a two-story space filled with plants, illuminated by a full roof skylight. In the middle was a green velvet couch with claw

69

feet and a carved mahogany back.

"I should have that couch," Helen said. "Do you think we can move it upstairs for the film?"

"I dunno, it looks pretty solid. Maybe when some of the other people arrive. We should film down here."

"I guess I can't really steal it because of the karma thing," Helen drawled.

We went back upstairs to get ready. Helen set up equipment, I took a bath and did my exercises. Just about the time I finished getting re-dressed, Helen went to answer the door.

Now I was nervous.

"This is Fritz."

Fritz had a slight dancer's body and a messy dark ponytail. He looked like he could live in the woods, either that or be an artist. But I already knew, Helen had told me he was a painter. He was wearing a white t-shirt.

"How d'you do?" I shook his hand, then turned to Helen. "Are you ready? Should I put on my make-up?"

"Yeah." She was already adjusting one of the lights.

"Let's go downstairs," Helen said. "Can you grab one of those candles, Fritz?"

"Wow, this is eerie," Fritz said when we were on the stairway.

Helen and I both giggled.

When we got downstairs, Helen told us to sit on the couch. Behind us were giant paintings turned to the wall, only the dirty white canvas and plywood struts showing. Tendrils of green hung down from the plants.

"I think there's enough light in here. Are you ready?"

I was shaking. So was Fritz. He had his head bowed and his hand up on his chest.

"I'm totally terrified and freaked out by this," I said to him.

"Oh?" he sounded surprised. Of course he didn't know me. He smiled gently and moved a little closer on the couch.

"Okay, let's go," Helen said.

I started the story.

"My cousin Dirk is a psychopathic criminal. He's a liar and a thief. He steals from people, but not in any way where he could actually get in legal trouble. Dirk is quite glamorous. His suits are all tailored and he has three or four hundred pairs of shoes. What he does is borrow money from people and never pay it back. Usually around fifteen or twenty thousand. And these are all people to whom that amount

of money is an annoyance but not enough to bother with the police. Also, at any given time he has his mother suing three or four people and then he takes that money too. Once my father came to town and bought Dirk's car, a fancy BMW, 750 SEL or something, and when my father sent the check, Dirk deposited it in the bank right when he knew the IRS was putting a lien on his account. Then, when the people to whom Dirk still owed money for the car asked him, Dirk said my father was now responsible for the payments."

Then I turned toward Fritz and started kissing him. It was hard to do; it wasn't fun because I was so nervous. I could feel Fritz still shaking.

"Cut," Helen said.

"Whew, this is difficult because I'm so frightened." I looked at my hands. Fritz looked sympathetic. "Do you want to stop?"

"No, I'm totally scared, but I want the finished picture," I said, talking down into my lap. "A lot of stuff that totally frightens me turns out to be the best stuff. Are you okay?" I asked him.

"Yeah, I'm scared, too, but I think it's okay. I feel better that you're so scared."

"You're all right with this? You don't feel like we're using you?"

"No. Why? Are you?"

"Yeah, sort of. Part of my idea is to use the kissing as a timing device, like I used to love this thing when I was waitressing. I would be telling someone a story, and it would start, 'I have a cousin who is a psychopath,' and then I'd run off and wait on table number 11 and then I'd come back and say, 'It's no wonder he was so fucked up, his mother had affairs with all of his father's best friends, including the head priest at Loyola,' and then I would go ring up a check." I made motions with my fingers as if I were ringing numbers on a cash register.

Fritz laughed. "Yeah. So what other ideas do you have about what this is?"

"Well, it's partly about glamour. The idea, especially in New York City, that having a boyfriend is not to have someone to be intimate with, it's to have someone who looks glamorous walking down the street with you. And people don't want to know, 'Do you love him?' they want to know, 'What does he do?' Like, it's good to be able to say, 'He's a deal maker at Paramount,' or, 'He's an artist with Pace.'"

"Right. Yeah. That's great." Fritz lowered his eyelids and smiled shyly. He looked like an angel.

"Okay. Ready," Helen said.

I continued telling the story.

"But he was the most incredibly glamorous person and when you were with him you felt like you had arrived. The rest of the world didn't matter. If Dirk accepted you, you had made it to the most secret of inner circles."

I turned to Fritz and touched his neck and face, then back to the camera. "I never come the first time I fuck someone. I'm too nervous, too busy thinking about what's going on."

And then we kissed more and suddenly it was great. I liked the way Fritz smiled. The way the hair traced the shy, elegant curve of his neck. All of a sudden it was as if we were in love. As we moved around the basement making the movie, I would walk by Fritz a little too close and I could hear him sigh slightly, and pretty soon when the camera stopped rolling, Fritz and I would go right on kissing.

"Hey, Helen," Fritz said. "I like kissing your friend June."

"Everyone wants to kiss June," Helen said, still filming.

"Oh yeah," I waved my hand airily. "My mother wants to kiss me, my father wants to kiss me . . ."

Fritz drew back a little and looked hurt.

"No," I said, instantly moving forward. "I'm joking. The kissing wasn't even my idea, it was Helen's. I had a different idea."

"What was your idea?" Fritz asked.

"Sex," I said.

Fritz looked at the floor, frowned, then looked up at me. "Okay," he said.

Helen and I both smiled.

"Let's go upstairs," Helen said.

Fritz and I were fooling around more. Fritz was taking off the velvet dress. I was pulling it back down, playing, teasing him.

Then we were on Helen's brass bed. We had no clothes on and Helen was filming. It was the most normal thing in the world.

"You know that thing you said?" Fritz asked me.

"What?"

"When you were talking about having sex and you said you never come the first time?"

"Yeah?"

"Well, it's like that for me too. Lots of times I can't even get excited, I'm so nervous. Though today . . ."

I laughed. "Must be because of the camera."

"Mims is coming pretty soon," Helen said.

I looked at Fritz. We hadn't really quite actually fucked, though we'd been

72

as close as you could possibly get. I was excited, but in a way I didn't want it to happen. I was worried about whether we should use a condom. I'd been secretly thinking about this all week. Mims' imminent arrival solved a lot of problems. I had to alter my thinking. I had to make myself stop desiring him.

We got up and put our clothes back on. Soon there was another voice outside yelling for Helen.

"Do you think you'll be jealous?" Helen asked Fritz as she headed for the door.

"Yes, I think so," he said. When she was in the hallway he said to me, "I'm supposed to go to this big party out on Long Island today, but maybe I should stay here for the rest of this."

"That would be okay." I looked at him. "But are you sure it'd be all right, really, for you to see me kissing other people? I don't know. It seems like I'm going to feel like I'm being unfaithful to you. Maybe you shouldn't stay. If you're here I might be more restrained." I straddled a chair, leaning my chest on the back. Mims sat on the bed talking to Helen. Fritz leaned forward, strong arms on his knees, from where he sat on a red velvet couch. The early afternoon sun filtered through the window and made light patterns on his face.

Going Out in the Middle of the Movie

"Well, have you ever done any actual, you know, prostitution?" Mims asked.

I smiled.

"I love this story," Helen said.

"But everyone already knows the story."

"I don't," said Fritz.

"Well, it was just that I was working at a bakery and this guy offered me fifty dollars to fuck him."

"And you said yes."

"Of course at first I said no, but he was working with me and to tell you the truth I didn't mind him." I paused. "And I was very poor."

"That's it? That's all that happened?" Fritz asked.

"No, no," Helen said from behind the camera, "tell him about the peanut butter."

I laughed. "Right, yeah. He gave me thirty dollars and told me he'd pay the rest later, which of course he never did. But I bugged him and bugged him, so finally he gave me an institutional-sized can of peanut butter. It was sort of good. My friend Lucy and I lived on it for a couple of weeks."

"So how'd it happen? How'd you do it? Did he want perverted stuff?"

"No, no, not on the sex part, that was completely normal, but he wanted to pretend to pick me up while I looked in the window of a sporting goods store dressed as a little girl." I laughed again. "Which was not that hard. I was only nineteen at the time."

"Okay, time to film," Helen said.

Kissing Mims was sort of like kissing a mannequin. She held real still and her body was unbelievably firm. At first I had a hard time with her nose. It reminded me of how I used to wonder when I was young watching people kiss on TV, how did they know what to do with their noses?

"Fritz?"

He jumped. Helen's question had startled him.

"Yes."

"I want you to pace back and forth behind them."

I was trying to make kissing Mims real like it had been with Fritz, but she wouldn't relax. Maybe it was because she was kissing another girl.

"Right after this I'm going to have to go," Helen began talking rapidly. "June, maybe you could go get more film. I'll leave you my bank card. The code is 4739. I'll write it down. You'll be back first, so I'm leaving the keys, too. Fritz and Mims, thank you very much for coming. I'll talk to you later. A little more kissing, I have about thirty seconds left. June, can you do me a quick version of the Horst thing."

I broke away from Mims.

"He was lovers with Horst P. Horst, they traveled all over the world. In Paris, my cousin would buy suits at the couture houses and charge them back to the hotel, I think it was the George V. They went to parties with Lee Radziwell and her sister. Dirk had a cocker spaniel from one of the Woolworth heiresses."

"Good." Helen turned off the camera, jumped off the chair, put the camera down and ran out the door.

I felt dazed. Now what should I do? In someone else's home with two lovers I didn't really know?

"Would you like some tea—or soup?"

"I'd love some soup," Mims said.

74

"What're you going to do now?" Fritz asked me.

"I'm going to get film. What's a good place?"

"You could go to E. Nunz's. They have good film."

"I hate that place," Mims said. "Every time I've ever been there they've been rude to me and their prices are high."

"Where else could she go?"

"Price's."

"But they're way over on West 23rd." Fritz paused. "I suppose I could drive you over," he said.

"You have a car?" Mims and I spoke in unison.

Fritz smiled. "Yeah, I brought it so I could go right to the party. And I think I will go, but if you want, June, I could give you a ride to get the film and back here."

"I'd like that."

"How many people does Helen have for you to kiss?" Fritz asked.

"I don't know. She told me this morning she had a few people lined up."

"I think it's more than a few," Mims said. "She had a list at work and it was a lot of people. Like, a yellow legal-sized notepad with names from the top of the page to the bottom. I'll bet it's around here." She looked around on Helen's desk. "Oh yeah, here it is." She was looking at the notepad and counting. "It looks like at least eight. There're more names on the list, but I see eight 'OKs.'"

I felt faint. It was so intense. What if I fell in love eight times like I did with Fritz? By the end of the day I'd be exhausted.

The three of us went out the door and walked over to Fritz's car. It was steaming hot in the streets now.

Fritz's car was roasting. We had to open all the doors and stand around on the sidewalk for a minute.

At 12th Street and Third Avenue the streets were jammed with cars, horns honking, heat shimmering off the pavement, so we changed our minds about Fritz taking me. Instead Fritz let Mims and me out on 15th Street near the Farmer's Market. I kissed him good-bye. There were trucks parked closely together, all piled high with zucchini, apples, cabbages, oranges, carrots, corn, and other ripe, glistening produce. One rusty truck was covered by a riot of perennials. I was happy because then I could be alone with Mims, so it was more like she was my second lover instead of just a quickie during Fritz.

"What are you doing this summer?" she asked me.

I was surprised, though this was a normal New York question like, "Where do you live?" A New Yorker can tell your entire life history if you tell them what street you live on. "Actually, I'm leaving for New Mexico on Tuesday."

"When are you coming back?"

"The beginning of September."

"That's great."

"Well, you know." I was a little embarrassed. "Usually it's rich people who manage this and I don't know how I've done it even though I'm totally poverty-stricken."

She hugged me. "Don't worry about that."

"What about you this summer?"

"I'm going to Greece."

"Wow, that's great."

She smiled. We had walked to the end of the market.

"Okay, bye," she said and kissed me.

I smiled and walked across the street then realized—I had absolutely no idea what I was doing. It was as if I had been picked up and put down in the middle of a strange planet. I had no idea how to get money. No idea where the camera store was. I didn't even know how to make my way back to Helen's house, even though I'd been there plenty of times. It was too confusing to be out of the movie.

I kept walking and of course then I remembered what to do. Just as I was coming to my senses I saw the E. Nunz film store. I went in.

"How much is Super 8 with sound?"

"$15.95."

"Okay, I'll be right back."

I knew where a bank of mine was, very close, so I went down there and got forty dollars.

"How much time on each roll?"

"3.2 minutes," said the very handsome young man with dark skin and a glossy ponytail.

"3.2 minutes? Oh dear, that doesn't seem like much time. Well, give me two with sound and two without."

He wrote it out. "That'll be $52.40."

I started putting my money on the table. I only had $51.00. "Oh, heavens." We both stood there.

"Is there any way . . ."

"I'll tell you what—" he said, at the same time calling to the back, "George, she's a dollar forty short on fifty two dollars worth of film."

"I'll bring it another day," I said.

"She'll bring it another day."
"Sure," came from the back.

About three blocks later I decided that wasn't enough film. Not considering that list of people. I found one of Helen's banks and tried her card. It didn't seem to work. I went back to my bank and took out sixty dollars, then went back to E. Nunz's.

"Hi."
"You're back."
"Yeah, I got more money."
"So you really *are* making a movie."
"Yeah."
"What's it about?"
"Well," I frowned. "It's about glamour." I paused for a moment, as if hesitating whether to tell him or not. "Actually it's me having sex with someone I never met before while I tell the story of my psychotic cousin."

His eyes widened. "I'd like to see that."
"I don't know. I think that this movie will be one of those kinds of movies that only fifteen or twenty East Village art people ever see."

"Oh."
I laughed. "I'd like two more rolls with sound and two without and of course I owe you a dollar forty."

I smiled and walked out on the street. I knew I looked wonderful, my hair shining, the velvet cocktail dress, the million gold necklaces glinting, black stockings with holes and tennis shoes. Every person looked at me. I felt great.

Outside

I saw two rock star guys, tight red jeans on one, black on the other, long thin legs, heavy metal hair down the middle of their backs, beautiful strong faces, and they were happy too, looking at me. I imagined they wanted me to be their rock star girlfriend.

Coming toward me were two rough guys. They would look too, I knew. They were the kind of guys who always mentally undressed you even if you had breasts that rested on your stomach. Maybe especially then, I thought.

One was fat with a t-shirt that didn't reach his jeans, the other was acned and

77

badly shaven.

I saw the fat one was purposefully not moving out of the way. I didn't change my path either; I was too happy, and paying more attention to the pretty rock stars. But when the tough guys got close I started to move.

"Excuse me," I said.

Suddenly the fat one grabbed for my breast.

I jumped back with a sharp intake of breath, terrified. "Oh." I'd forgotten, guys like this wanted to destroy anything they couldn't have.

Out of the corner of my eye I sensed that the two rock stars also saw and were shocked. Should they, would they have to come get in a fight? They had been staring, which in a way made me belong to them. But they were the type of guys who had opted out of violence years ago, much preferring marijuana, loud sound and wild girls.

Then I was halfway down the block; the rough guys were confused and couldn't come after me fast enough before I turned the corner. I remembered again why I liked to hide when I went outside.

I went back to Helen's, took another shower, and did more yoga.

"June, hey June." It was Helen calling from outside, back from her class.

"How was the thing?" I asked her.

"Stupid. I shouldn't have gone. Did you find the film?"

"It's in that bag. Wow. I didn't realize it was so expensive."

"Yeah." She looked in the bag. "Jesus June, you don't fool around. This is great."

"I was worried we'd run out."

"Did I tell you the story of Fritz and Mims?"

"No. You mean together? I noticed they knew each other."

"This is good. Fritz and Mims were lovers at Skowhegan—you know, it's an art camp—eighteen years ago, and Fritz was madly in love with Mims and she was deeply mean to him. I mean she iced him bigger than ever in history before."

"Oh my."

"Right. Then, get this, they have had absolutely nothing to do with each other for eighteen years. If Mims heard that he would be at a party, she wouldn't go. Until about three months ago, my friend Santana threw a party and she went and they talked the entire time. But I guess stuff is still weird."

"Man, that's unbelievable. I had no idea. Of course. So that's why you asked Fritz if he would be jealous. You meant both ways."

Helen laughed that deep, throaty, almost evil chuckle.

Get Ready June, the Movie's Starting Again

"Dave is next," Helen told me.

"He's the one you told me built your cabinets, right?"

She turned toward the door. "Oh, there he is."

Dave was a bicycle guy. Thick, curly, long black hair, tight spandex shorts, a matching tight shirt, and a baseball cap with the short rim flipped back. Thick muscles in his legs.

We sat on the bed. I started telling the Dirk story again.

"It's not surprising that he was so fucked up, his mother slept with every one of my uncle's best friends, including the head priest at Loyola. In the divorce proceedings all of my uncle's friends came to him and said they were willing to testify so he could get custody of the kids, and my uncle said he didn't want his friends' reputations to be ruined.

Sometimes when the kids came home from the school they attended, a very expensive private school in Wilmette—New Trier—, my aunt would call and say that she couldn't make dinner because she was at '21' with one of her lovers. They lived in Chicago! Or they would come home in the afternoon to find her passed out on the lawn. Once, dead drunk, she tried to climb into bed with Dirk.

She was a top model, on the cover of Life magazine, every winter she would go down to Florida for the spring shows and mostly leave the kids at home with my uncle. Sometimes she took Dirk, he was her pet, not that that was any advantage. Once she insisted on traveling even though he had a temperature of 103."

I turned to kiss David. He pecked hard at me, lips stiff. It was about as romantic as getting your knee reflexes tested. I tried softening up myself. No good.

"You must really hate this," I said to him.

"No, no, oh no," he reassured me, but I didn't believe him.

"Stay here a minute," I said and lay back, beside him but not touching him. "Have you known Helen a long time?"

He grinned and lay back too. I rolled around on my stomach and propped my chin on my hands.

"Long. Yes. I think I met her the first week she was in New York."

"Are you from here?"

"Yeah. I grew up in Little Italy. My grandparents lived in the house next door to us."

"That must have been good."

He looked surprised. "Yes, it was, but growing up in New York was rough. It was already rough then."

"What about meeting Helen?" I asked.

"She got me to help her carry home this enormous plaster sculpture of an angel she found on the street. I was just walking along and she yelled, 'Hey you' at me. You know, and she was waving her arms around really wildly. I'm not sure why I stopped, probably just shocked, but she talked a lot on the way home and so I became her friend. Helen had just moved here. That was right before I met my girlfriend."

"The girlfriend you have now?" I was incredulous.

"Yes."

"But didn't Helen move here a long time ago?"

"Nine years. I've had the same girlfriend for almost nine years."

"Wow. Did you ever think of marrying her?" I hurriedly amended, "Not that I'm in favor of marriage."

"*She* wants to be married." David did not sound happy.

"Yeah well, that's a problem. You don't?"

"I don't know."

So that's what had been wrong with his kissing.

"You sort of want to?" Now that he was talking about his life, I relaxed.

"It's the problem of freedom. I always get so confused. First I want security, and I love her, but then I feel claustrophobic and I want my freedom. Work's the same problem."

"Helen told me you do carpentry."

"Sometimes, but I also work for my girlfriend's father. He manufactures stoves in Brooklyn. It's a big business and I could be very secure. I know he wants me to eventually take over the business, you know, he has only one son who works for a hotel in Florida, but I don't know. I think I'd rather do free-lance carpentry and ride my bike. I'm not sure."

Helen had been putting more film in the camera on the other side of the room, but evidently she heard this last remark. "Have you been riding a lot?"

David visibly brightened. "I rode to Montauk yesterday. It was beautiful. I'd like to live on a beach."

I felt sad. "Maybe you should leave your girlfriend."

"But I love her." He looked tortured.

Helen walked over, and was about to say something when we heard someone calling her name. Her head swung in the direction of the door. "Probably

Andrew. I don't know if we can get him to kiss you, but he did say he'd bring some sound equipment." She went to let him in.

Andrew Had Been Helen's Boyfriend for Five Years

Helen introduced us but Andrew didn't look at me. She began discussing the sound problem with him. "There's so much background noise in here I don't know if I've gotten anything at all on the soundtrack. I tried closing the windows and blinds, but you know this neighborhood."

She stopped talking. We could all hear salsa music, yelling, and the roar of a motorcycle.

"Okay, can I just read the script once into the tape recorder? I'd like that. I feel like I should have memorized it," I asked.

"That's not what I think," said Helen. "I think you're sticking too close to it."

"Really?"

"You can read it through. I don't know yet what I'll do with all the stuff."

"Let's try it in the bathroom," Andrew said.

Andrew was quite handsome; a strong tall body and a long face with full cheeks. He had pouty lips and a slightly hooked nose, and dark curly hair.

He and Helen went into the bathroom. I was looking in my purple bag for the script. I saw David was still sitting over on the bed.

"C'mere," I motioned to him. "You should come in the bathroom with us. You could help me by holding the pages after I'm finished with them. You know, the microphone will pick up the sound of paper rustling unless we're careful."

"Okay."

It was crowded in the bathroom with the four of us. David and I sat on the edge of the bathtub, I held the pages apart with my fingers and David carefully took them when I was finished. Helen stood motionless, leaning against the wall with her arms folded.

"Okay," Andrew said.

I started again, "My cousin . . ."

When I stopped Andrew clicked off the machine.

"I was a soundman last weekend too. I guess it's my new job. I'm not sure how it happened." He laughed. "I better be careful though, not only doesn't it pay as well as my regular job, I even like it less."

Helen had left the bathroom and set up the camera on a tripod facing a long green velvet drape just outside the door. "Andrew, come here," she called. "Stand right against the wall."

He stood there.

"June."

I went over and kissed Andrew. He was tall so I had to stand up on my toes. His lips were soft, but he seemed frightened.

"Don't worry," Helen said. "This will only take a minute."

I could hear the camera going.

"Okay, that's enough," she said.

Andrew looked stunned.

The Second Most Beautiful Man

"Here's Richard," Helen said, making him materialize, I hadn't heard any sounds of a new arrival.

He was very tall, maybe six-foot-four, and beautiful. A chin with an exact strength—no cleft, more perfect than if it had had a cleft—and dark eyes and long, smooth, chestnut hair.

"Go ahead," Helen said, then, "Wait, wait. June could you stand on a chair?"

I was relieved. I needed something to stand on to kiss Richard. Suddenly I was taller than him. He was nervous.

Richard was someone who under certain circumstances I could really enjoy kissing so I wanted him to like it. But it was over too quickly. I couldn't get him to relax.

(Maybe Fritz was the only one who got turned on because that was the only time I was scared. We were equal.)

I asked him to sit down and sat on his lap. I didn't want to lose the body contact before a rapport was established.

"Did you grow up in New York?" I asked him.

"No. Did you?"

"No. I grew up on a piece of land on the coast of California. My father hated the Fifties, hated the McCarthy hearings, the hypocritical sexuality of Doris Day and Donna Reed, the glorification of the advertising man, so he bought a piece of property far away from anyone else and kept us isolated. I grew up building forts with my brothers."

"It sounds great."

"It would have been if the family was as perfect as they thought they were."

"Would I like your father? It sounds like I would like him."

I looked at him appraisingly. I knew so little about him. He'd been an intern at *GQ*, working for Helen. She hadn't thought he'd come for the movie, but he had.

"Yes, I think you would like him. He's very funny, witty, and he can remember lots of amazing things. Facts about the Galapagos turtles, the War of the Roses, or how a television is built. He's incredibly honest, silly and dignified at the same time. He wishes sometimes that he had been a forest ranger instead."

"I'm pretty sure I'd like him," Richard said wistfully. "Tell me more."

"He dresses country elegant. He has perfect suits that he's had for thirty-five years. Maybe you'll see him in an incredibly silly pair of patchwork pants and then the next week in *Town & Country* all the men are wearing them." I giggled remembering. "When he works in the garden he wears this shirt with a million holes that he's worn since forever. What does your father do?"

"He's retired. He was in the diplomatic corps."

"Where does he live?"

"Gallup, New Mexico."

"Gallup, New Mexico?! Wow, that's a wild choice. You know Gallup, New Mexico is filled with drunken Indians. On the edge of town there is—though I don't know if they have it anymore—a field with a fence around it where a sheriff and his deputies take all the drunk Indians at night and in the mornings they walk back to the reservation. It's a strange place to pick to live."

"He's only lived there a couple of years. Before that he lived in San Jose."

"He got sent to San Jose with the diplomatic corps?!!" I could hardly imagine.

"No, that was right after he retired."

"Your father must be a strange man to pick those two places out of anywhere on earth. What about your mother, where does she live?"

"Denmark. She's Danish."

"Do you see her much?"

"No. I haven't seen either of them in five years."

Dark Red Brocaded Velvet

Helen's apartment was soft at the edges, like velvet, and full of cameras and microphones and lights in the center. Like a jewel-case. And I would be in the center with someone, shining like diamonds.

One person after another, each of them more amazing than the one before or at least as amazing. In the room, the person would come in—Andrew, David, Richard, Mims—the person and I would be in the center of this golden light, kissing and kissing and kissing, with others on the edges, in the shadows of the room. All beautiful, exquisitely formed. And this went on and on and on.

Girl

Oh no. I looked up and there was Nicki, just barely in my field of vision, on the edge of the lights. Standing out from the hazy darkness and the dim shapes of furniture that inhabited Helen's apartment, Nicki looked golden.

She stepped forward, walking to center stage, oblivious to me. I stepped out of the way.

"Hi, Nicki."

"Here. You want some?"

She handed me a bottle I assumed was ginger ale, which I never drink but decided a small gulp wouldn't hurt me today, but it was beer. I was momentarily shocked. Nicki stood in the middle of the lights. Her hair was very blonde and short, sticking out straw-like, Darryl Hannah in *Blade Runner*. Her eyelashes were gold and her face shone gold too. Her square mouth and feral teeth looked dangerous. She was wearing a white shirt and high black pants with only the slightest hint of the long strong thighs underneath.

I walked over closer to her.

"You look beautiful."

She stood straight and looked at the camera. "Sometimes I like to do that." She smiled but not at me.

"You aren't going to kiss me, are you?" she asked.

"Why not?" and I went over and kissed her on the cheek then across her face, three, four kisses, then on her mouth.

"Yech, not on my mouth." She spit and pushed me away.

I laughed and got off the stage, letting her have it for a while.

84

More

"June," Helen ordered, "go get Daniel." She pronounced it "Dan-yell."

I was semi-aware that she had made everyone go out on the porch, but not that anyone new had arrived. I'd been too busy paying attention to Nicki.

I went outside. It was extra-dark after the movie lights.

"Dan-yell."

A tall man unfolded himself from the stoop.

This one is different, I thought.

"Oh no," a deep male voice said. "It's like being called into the principal's office."

Inside, right away, I wanted to order him around, make requests.

"Lie down on the floor, okay?"

When he lay down I got on top and began kissing him. I could hear the whirr of the camera, knew you couldn't see anything because my hair was falling between our faces.

I sat up to look at the camera.

"He was lovers with Horst P. Horst and they would fly all over the world, staying in magnificent hotels. Dirk went to all the best parties in New York. He knew Andy Warhol. He told me this story once of going to a club, a nightclub, with a famous actor he'd met at the Factory and when you got inside, you checked your clothes, and the entire room was filled with the most beautiful men in the world. Models, more beautiful than models, all naked. Dirk had a cocker spaniel from one of the Woolworth heiresses."

I kissed Daniel again. *"He burnt down my parents' house, but that was an accident, I'm sure it was an accident . . ."*

Helen had kept Andrew in the room. He was recording the sound, holding the microphone close to our faces. "What do you think?" Helen was behind the camera but I knew she was talking to me. "Daniel is different."

"I'm tired," I said to him. "You tell me a story."

"What kind?" Daniel asked.

He smiled at me. He had a long thin mobile face and heavy eyebrows.

I smiled back and looked at Helen. "Can we make him take his clothes off?"

"I don't think you can *make* Daniel do anything," she said.

"Okay. Daniel, will you please take your clothes off?"

85

"All of them?" he asked. "Can I keep on my socks?"

I laughed. I knew he'd take them off, too.

I had to get up off of Daniel, which left Andrew the closest person to him while he was undressing. As he did it, I looked at his penis.

"Okay. I know. You tell a story and I'll repeat it," Daniel said.

"All right, when I was young, going to a very small parochial school, I was very quiet and good. One day we were sitting in class and I happened to notice that it had gotten windy outside, very very windy. I assumed the teacher would also notice because it was clear to me that it was the windiest day ever before or since. After a minute I raised my hand and asked, wasn't she going to let us go out? She was surprised and said no."

Daniel thought for one second. "Okay. I went to my cousin's wedding and I arrived late. My uncle, who is a big windbag, was on the front porch, and he trapped me. I begged him to let me go in, but he was drunk and kept me there for two hours." He smiled at me expectantly.

"All right. I was on a train in Spain. My only contact with the English language was the book *Ulysses*, and my brain was very tired. There were some soldiers who promised to wake me when we got to Madrid. In the middle of the night there was a horrible screeching and when I woke up the soldiers were hurriedly getting their rucksacks down and they left. I was panicked and desperately tried to wake up as I collected my stuff, believing we were in the station. Seconds later the police came in, with much clanking of metal, searched the whole compartment, and left. Out the window was not the city, but empty fields extending as far as I could see."

"Mmmm. I was cleaning a stain on the windowpane of my friend's new house. We were moving slowly because of the arduousness of the task. I fell asleep in front of the TV after a time and he awakened me and we resumed work. He gave me a beer."

I sighed. This was a little too intense for me.

Helen said, "Hold it for one second."

"It's like a diversion of Walter Abish, isn't it?" Andrew asked.

Daniel laughed. "If it were triple-rooted through Bataille, maybe. Who else would do something like this? Maybe Jarry, but in French. La pluie en Espagne pleut surtout sur la plaine."

"Bien, j'adore la traduction sans rhyme," said Andrew ironically.

Everyone laughed.

"Time for Suzanne."

Suzanne came in.

"Let's go in the bathroom," Helen said.

I was tired now—or rather, completely relaxed. I had decided to reapply my lipstick for each person, which meant I also had to fix the foundation around my mouth.

Suzanne was sitting on the toilet. I was leaning against the sink. I felt the sex thing. She was so beautiful. Tall and willowy with a heart-shaped face and green eyes.

I remember she told me one time that her hair would be completely gray if she didn't dye it, and I was amazed. That's another interesting thing I realized: All the women had met me before, none of the men had. It made sense. You could imagine a director calling a guy on the phone and saying, "Hey, wanna be in a movie? All you gotta do is just come over and kiss my friend," and the guys would go, "Hey sure." But women would have to have an exact idea of the physical presence before they'd agree to kiss another woman.

I wanted to kiss her strongly, passionately, put my hand behind her head and pull her tight to me, but that's not how I am. I wouldn't take a chance on scaring her.

So I kissed her gently, stroked her shoulder, didn't get carried away.

She bit me just a little.

Afterward Helen sat on the bathtub to take the last roll of film out of the camera.

Suzanne lounged against the door frame.

"Helen?" Her voice sounded like a little girl's. "Can I try on your new rumble suit?" She wiggled her shoulders back and forth.

"It's okay with me, but it's dirty, under the bed."

"What's this?" Suzanne reached one slim finger out to barely hook a flimsy black garment hanging on the bathroom door.

"That's Darryl's old bathing suit. He looks great in them, but that one lost it's support, you know—" she laughed "—so he gave it to me."

"Oh." Suzanne looked disappointed. She wanted to try on the suit. I knew which one she meant; Helen had worn it one day when we were going to lunch. One piece, no sleeves, short pants, made out of incredibly flimsy light green silk with tiny holes. Helen had bought it at Yamamoto last month. Suzanne would look good in it, she's lanky like Helen. I have to stick pretty close to black cocktail dresses myself.

"No more film."

"Let's go outside," Helen said to me.

I would have agreed to anything she said.

Outside David, Andrew, Richard, and Daniel were sitting on the steps with Nicki.

"It doesn't matter how often they discover smaller particles," Nicki said. "They look, they say there's nothing there, then someone finds something, you know, the next thing, quarks, then a biton. The reason they find that stuff is because they look. See, they are not actually *finding* it, they're *inventing* it."

"Their twisted minds cause the particles to spring into being," Daniel intoned, half-mockingly.

I went and stood by the gate, Suzanne leaned against the stair railing, and Helen made Nicki move over on the steps. This is it, I thought. I have gotten where I want to be. I didn't need anything more than to be here on this warm late spring evening with these people telling jokes after having just finished making a movie.

We went to a Mexican restaurant with linoleum floors and a second formica table was pulled noisily over to accommodate us. The only people there besides us were the family of owners drinking coffee and waiting patiently until closing time when they could finish cleaning up. I ate rice.

Everyone Leaves, the Moon is Brilliant, Helen and I Are Alone

"Do you want to borrow some things to wear to sleep in?" Helen brought out white men's boxers and an undershirt. She was wearing the same thing. When we lay down on the bed, I sighed with happiness. I was content to have my skin inside the soft white cotton. Helen was smiling too.

"What do you think of Nicki?" Helen asked.

"You know, I don't think she likes me."

"No, no, no, she thinks you're great. She told me so after that first time you met her at one of Ginka's parties."

"Yeah, I know she liked me then, but after that I disappointed her. And today I don't think she saw why I was the star at all. Of course there was no good reason except for the fact that you and I thought of it and I wrote it."

"You knew she crashed. She wasn't invited."

"Really?" I giggled. "That's great."

"She just called everybody to see what was going on and they were all coming over here. I bet she was sort of annoyed there wasn't a hipper event to go to."

"She sure did look beautiful."

"She thought she was coming to an Andy Warhol Factory event."

"She hated me kissing her."

We both giggled.

"I was happy Nicki got to leave with the guys." I turned toward Helen.

"Yeah, that was good."

"I loved Fritz."

"Yeah, you two were so cute together I could hardly stand it." Helen stretched her arms up and yawned. "You should have an affair with him when you come back."

"Oh, do you think I could?"

"Yes, June, of course. But listen, there's something I've been meaning to ask you for about a month now and I keep forgetting."

We both drifted off into a half-sleep.

"What?" I remembered to ask her.

"I forgot again," she said. "It's strange, isn't it, when you think back on the people you associated with." Helen stretched out her long legs. "Like when I was in high school, my best friend was named Amy. She was the girlfriend of a big coke dealer and she would invite me over to the hotel where they lived together. You know, he was twenty-five or something, incredibly old. We would go to the room and take enormous amounts of drugs and jump up and down on the beds. She had the most beautiful long golden hair that would fly all around. I can't imagine where she is now."

"What about her boyfriend?"

"Oh, he got sent to jail not long after that. We were sort of in trouble too, but they let us off because we were so young."

"You know, Helen, the strangest thing—and I just realized it—is I have no idea what any of those people today thought of me. You know, usually I could tell you exactly. I remember when I went to Duke I would come home and tell Michael, my boyfriend, 'Oh, yeah, in chemistry, this guy named Dan sits next to me and he thinks I'm sort of crazy but he's interested in my stories, and next to him this guy Cliff, he thinks I might possibly be too weird and he knows there is something different about me but he hasn't quite put his finger on it, and Andrea, she has a crush on Dan and she's afraid I might steal . . .' I would pause for breath and Michael would say, 'June, this is your first week of class. Those people are worrying about how much homework they're going to have to do, they're not thinking about you.'"

Helen laughed. "But you were right, I bet. It only takes a second for some-one to develop a complex group of impressions."

I was talking and she went to sleep.

"Helen, I'm definitely in love with you, but I don't know about the sex part."

She smiled and woke up a little. "Don't worry about that, we've been having sex all day."

"Helen?"

"Yes."

I could tell she was almost asleep. "The other thing I was thinking about being gay is that if you think about it the people who say how bad it is are all people who've never tried it. Like, pretend that it's like apple pie and you have all these people circling around it, completely fascinated, but they wouldn't dare eat any. And they say, 'Don't eat that apple pie, it's terrible.' And you ask them, 'Have you ever tried it?' 'Oh no,' they say. 'It's too terrible for us to risk trying it.' It's weird, huh, Helen?"

"Uh huh." Helen murmured agreeably, her eyes closed.

Who Do I Meet Standing in Front of the Knitting Factory

"Juuune." I could hear how much he liked me in the way he drew out my name.

I had no idea who he was, but he looked vaguely familiar and very handsome.

He walked toward me. I was trying to remember.

"Why are you here?" he asked me.

"We went to a poetry reading." I indicated Henry, with whom I had come. "In there." I pointed stupidly at the door of the Knitting Factory, and it came to me who he was—Jake Hoving, the painter.

"You look different," I said. "Your beard and mustache are gone."

"Oh, yeah, maybe." He felt his chin with his hand.

"This is Henry. Henry, Jake. Henry Zemel. Jake Hoving." I was a lot more shaken now. It was one thing when I just thought it was an attractive guy who liked me, something completely different and much more nerve-wracking now that I realized it was Jake.

"Where are you living?" he asked.

"Uptown," I said, "but I'm going to New Mexico in five days."

"For how long?"

"The summer. You know, in New Mexico, everyone hugs me and hugs me and kisses me and kisses me."

90

His eyes flickered. "I might go in three weeks. A friend of mine is having an opening in Santa Fe July 13."

"Maybe we could meet." It was extremely difficult for me to talk, the desire to touch him was so strong. I felt like everything was in slow motion.

He raised his eyebrows. "He'll be at the Gerald Peters Gallery. Dirk Santor."

"Say it again."

He repeated it, looking directly at me.

"Okay, I'll go anyway."

"Yeah."

"I heard you were moving to Tribeca," I said.

"Yeah. Sam."

I knew he was referring to the fact that Sam had told him everything I'd said. "Oh, he talked to you." I could hardly breathe; I was amazed I was being so bold.

"He did."

We both stood there.

"I guess I better go," I said.

"Yeah, I'm waiting for someone." He made a movement in the air behind him. "But come here, I have to hug you and kiss you."

Henry and I went off to a hip restaurant. We got into an argument about the downtrodden. It was about three hours later that my body calmed down.

Seconds Before I Leave to Go to New Mexico

"I saw Daniel today."

"Where?"

"On the street."

"Did you talk to him?" Helen asked. She sounded like a little girl.

"No, I just saw him. You know, I'm leaving so soon that I didn't expect this to happen. I started smiling real hard because of course it's completely ridiculous to look across the street and think, 'Hey, there's the guy I was kissing in the movie on Saturday.' I waved to him and he waved back, he was smiling real big in exactly the same way. Then I went down Greene Street. I kept smiling and pretty soon everyone was smiling, a red-kerchiefed cleaning woman, a couple of truck drivers, some store clerks standing outside for a smoke."

"Hi, this is Junie Smith."

There was a pause on the other end of the line.

"June from the movie."

"Oh, June." He sounded really happy I'd called. "I never knew your last name. If you'd just said *the* June I would have known immediately."

I laughed. I thought he was great.

"When are you leaving?" he asked.

"Well, we were supposed to leave tonight, but the car broke. The radiator."

"You know, that happened to me the day we did the movie. The radiator exploded when I was on my way back from Long Island."

"What'd you do?" I was hoping I could find out what to do about our car.

"I had to just leave it and later I went back with a tow truck. It was pretty bad. I had to get a new one."

"Oh no. That's terrible. Do you think that's what will happen to us?"

He laughed at me. "Oh now I see where your concern lies. Don't worry. Usually it's pretty simple to fix the radiator. Was there any steam coming out of the cap?"

"Yes."

"Were you driving it for a long time in the heat?"

"Only a couple of hours."

"Today?"

"Yeah."

"It was pretty hot today. It probably just needs more fluid. You should check and make sure there isn't a leak in the hose."

I was going to start having a hard time talking to him on the phone, he was too cool. I was beginning to feel the impulse to shamelessly beg him to be my boyfriend.

Just then Michelle came in and threw down the AAA booklet. She was mad.

"We should call the people," she said loudly, not really making any concession for me being on the phone.

"Uh oh," I said to Fritz. "I think I'm going to have to get off the phone."

"This is a disaster." Michelle was almost yelling while she glared at me.

I spoke softly into the telephone. "I think I'm getting in trouble. I'll send you a postcard, though."

92

"You want my address?"

"Oh. Yes."

"Fritz Drake. Thirty nine and a half Morton Lane, 10029."

"I love halves. Have a nice time."

"Call me when you get back."

"Yes. Oh yes. I will." I had to hang up.

Call to Clare #13

"Where are you?" Clare asked. "I called your house yesterday and the phone was disconnected."

"I'm staying at Michelle's house. Tomorrow we're leaving for New Mexico. You know, we were supposed to go tonight, but the radiator broke. Anyway, it's all taken care of so we're leaving in the morning. How are you?"

"I'm a little sad about Sam today."

I sighed. "I know, it's too bad. You probably thought of the scenario, as I have, where you and Sam get together and because of your training you loosen up all of his addictions, allowing him to become a truly great artist and he sees you as beautiful, which pretty much cures your depression and—can I say this?—occasional abrasiveness, and the two of you travel the world together."

"Yeah, I thought of that."

I spoke completely monotone, hardly moving my mouth, frightened by the subject. "It's too bad it's not going to happen."

"Yeah." Clare had more of the sadness we were both feeling in her voice.

"And all because Sam is too afraid."

"You think that's it, huh?"

"I'm afraid so. By now he most likely does have another girlfriend, a young one who doesn't threaten him."

She sighed. "Well, probably things are going better in your life. Tell me, tell me about the men in New Mexico who are not afraid."

"Oh, my god," I exclaimed. "How would I know? I myself am terrified."

We both laughed.

"But I always tell people how courageous you are," she said.

"Me? No way. The main thing about me is that I am so afraid of everything it all becomes equal. It was so extremely frightening for me to leave my room and go to breakfast when I was young that I figured, once I'd done that, why not trek across North Africa by yourself?"

"I might just be sad about this other thing. Brian was murdered."

"*What?*!!"

"In Detroit."

"Oh my god, Clare. That's terrible. That's horrible. I'm so sorry. I feel terrible."

"Yeah. I've pretty much been in tears all week. I can't believe it. It just happened. Tomorrow I'm going to go pick up the body."

"You'll bring him back to Chicago?"

"Yeah, the state pays for that, at least."

"Wow, I'm sorry. I know how much he meant to you."

"It was a gang thing. I always told him those guys were serious. I guess he snuck out one night and didn't come back. They found him a couple of days later. You know, they'll never find who did it. No one cares."

"You do."

Clare's voice shook. "Yeah. Like I said, I've been crying a lot. My supervisor's been pretty nice though. I think she knew how I felt about him even before he left. She gave me the day off after I heard, and she's the one who arranged for me to go get him."

"Yeah."

"I feel terrible though. I knew it wasn't good for him to go to Detroit." She sighed. "I guess it's impossible."

"Yeah."

"I guess we better hang up now."

"Oh, Clare, don't you want to talk more?"

"No, it's okay. If I do I'll just start crying. Maybe I'll call up Terry and Dale and go hang out over at their house, watch a movie on the VCR. There's not too much I can do."

"All right. I'm deeply sorry."

"Yeah, okay. I hear ya. Bye."

In New Mexico

I walked up to the door. Loud music spilled out into the clear night. There was a blond boy with a mustache.

"Your ID please."

I had forgotten about this. Getting carded. I pulled off my sunglasses. "I'm thirty-five, almost thirty-six." I smiled.

"Okay," he said amiably and waved me in.

A girl with masses of kinky curly hair, very brown skin and small breasts took my money, then I sauntered down the black-lighted hallway to a packed bar. House music thumped heavily. Great. I was turned on. White shirts glowed in the dark, the young boys all had sleek ponytails, Indian and Hispanic blood, dark eyes. I walked forward. I just wanted sex. I waited. The bartender was beautiful—round face, baseball cap, strong thighs, blue eyes looking directly at me, a gold earring. "What can I do for you?"

"A soda," I said, but wanted to yell, "No, no, I don't want a soda. I want to touch you, I want to push you down, feel my muscles tighten around you, whisper sex things in your ear."

But of course I didn't. Of course.

I walked to the next room, graffiti splashed all over the walls, neon colors, a loud punk band, girls in white spandex tops, bright next to dark skin, smooth young flesh.

Back into the dance room. I started dancing. I reached the point where I didn't care, sweaty, great music.

I went upstairs for a break. I could feel the strands of curls stuck to my shiny neck and throat. My arms glistened.

Androgyny, maybe that's the thing, I thought. Women who look like men. I myself liked women who looked like men and men who looked like women. It was the shock I liked, kissing soft lips, then surprise, he's got a big hard cock.

It Shouldn't Really Have Come as a Big Surprise that Mr. Sackler Was There at the 99 Club

I saw him sitting in the corner of the bar with his same great, black, horn-rimmed glasses and was happy. I would have been happy to see any person I hadn't seen in awhile. I forgot so easily.

He indicated that I should come over and sit on the bar stool next to him.

"How've you been June? I thought you'd moved to New York or something."

"I did. I do live in New York. I just came back for the summer to write a book. How have you been?"

"Pretty good. About the same. Tired. I got up this morning at six-thirty. You know my son owns this bar."

"Yeah. I did. You have a lot of children, right?"

He laughed. "In World War Two I was drafted. Afterwards I got married. My parents had died so I didn't have any relations. My wife and I had a lot of children." He looked contemplative. "My oldest three daughters live in California . . ."

"Oh yeah, what're they like?"

He laughed. "Well, the two oldest have each been married three times."

"Wow, three times."

"My oldest daughter is a psychiatrist. And all of her husbands have been psychiatrists. The first two were New York Jews . . ."

"Oh, yeah," I interrupted, laughing. "I have a weakness for them myself."

"Her last husband is a psychiatrist, too."

"What about the rest of your kids?"

"Well, Ariana, the youngest, just graduated from high school."

"Yeah, your girls were all so beautiful."

He looked thoughtful again. "That's right. All my kids are good-looking. Ariana has a hard time, you know she got pregnant in high school. Her son Darien is five. It took her five years, but she's through and thinking about going to UNM."

"Yeah, uh huh, that's good."

The bartender came over.

"Need anything, Mr. Sackler?"

"Can I buy you a drink, June?" He introduced me to the bartender. "June, this is Jerry."

"Hi," I said. "I'd love a soda."

Mr. Sackler ordered a tonic for himself.

"I had a problem with my heart and had to give up drinking."

"Was it hard?"

"No, not really. It doesn't matter."

"Well, I don't drink either," I said. "I just got up one day and I was tired of it."

"Do you like to watch TV?"

I wrinkled my face. "Well, yes, I do, yes. I don't get to very often, it's hard for me to remember to do it."

"I watch a lot of TV. I don't sleep much these days."

"Really? Does that happen to everyone?"

96

"It seems to. Last night I went to sleep about two."

"And what time did you get up?" But as soon as the words left my mouth I remembered he had told me already—six-thirty. Oh well.

"Six-thirty. Do you want to come over to my house to watch TV?"

"Well, I don't think so, not tonight. Maybe some other time."

"It'll have to be in July then. I only have tonight. My wife's out of town and she won't be gone again until July."

"Where'd she go?"

"She's at a wedding in Texas."

"Oh. It's quite nice of you to offer." I looked at him. I couldn't imagine kissing him. It didn't seem like it was because of his age; there were some perfectly beautiful young men I had looked at and decided the same thing.

I thought for a minute. I didn't feel the same as the last time he asked, when I'd been tempted to fuck him for money and ashamed. "Listen, before, you know, when we were going to go look at the house, I was embarrassed." I pointed at my chest. "I was embarrassed to myself."

He looked at me. "I need a companion. And I don't know how to do it. "

"Oh." To me it was a lot different if I was the only one. I had thought he went through a series of waitresses, flirting, then offering them money. It certainly happened at the country club often enough, everyone knew it. "Oh, my, I don't know."

"I don't have anyone to talk to."

"I don't think I'm the right person. But maybe I can think of where you can find someone. Let me think about it."

"My wife is a devout Catholic." He was looking straight ahead, as if just reminiscing to himself. "Goes to Mass four times a week, is incessantly saying novenas. She's done this since she was in the fifth grade. We live platonically. Every time I slept with her she got pregnant. I haven't slept with her in ten years. And probably not seven times in the last twenty."

"Oh, yeah, that's too bad."

"I didn't know. When I was eighteen, I got drafted. I'd had a year and a half of college. I was in the army three years and when I got out I married her."

"Yeah, hmmmm." I thought for a minute. Honestly, I didn't know what to say. "Do you like her?"

"Yeah, I like her. We don't have much in common. She's been arrested six times in the last couple of years for demonstrating at abortion clinics."

"Oh."

"You know Bobby Marchieta? He gets her out. He's pro-abortion, but we've been friends for forty years."

97

"**Hi, Dad,** how's it going?"

"Pretty good." Mr. Sackler nodded out in the direction of the general club. "Pretty busy tonight."

Mark grinned. "We're always like this."

Mr. Sackler turned to me while he looked at Mark. "You remember meeting June?"

"Of course I remember her," he said, with a small hint of annoyance at his father for implying he wouldn't remember. He smiled at me. "I thought you moved."

"I did. I'm here for the summer. I live in New York."

"I've never been to New York." He looked straight in my eyes.

"You should go there," I said. "It's very glamorous."

"I had a job once where we were supposed to go, but the district manager kept fucking up and finally the whole thing fell apart."

I know he thought I wasn't listening. In fact it was hard; he hadn't broken eye contact. He had changed, and also gotten incredibly handsome.

He started talking to his Dad and I did stop paying attention. I could have listened, but I was too lazy and it seemed like I would just have to pretend to be fascinated (the surfer girlfriend thing: While the guys demonstrate their incredible skill, the girls stand on the beach in tiny bikinis and watch). It was more fun to scan the room.

I once went on a blind date with Mark, the weirdest blind date in the world. One day, right after I started working at the country club, I was waiting on these men and they said, "You're awfully young to be working here, aren't you?" and I said, "I guess I am." And then they said, "And thin, too," and I laughed. Then they said, "Do you have a boyfriend?" and I said "No," so they all started talking real loud about how they were going to have to get me a good one, and the men at the next table said, "Hey wait a minute, why don't you pay attention to us? We could get you a boyfriend too." Well I was having the greatest time, I even forgot I was waitressing. I had to go in the back and calm down.

Not much ever came of it, but Mr. Sackler, who had been one of the men, evidently didn't forget, and the next time I waited on him he suggested I go out with his son.

"He's a DJ," he said.

98

"Oh yeah? I like DJ's. How old is he?"

"Twenty-four."

"I think that's too young."

"He's old for his age. Mature."

"Still." I laughed and ran off to another table.

After that, periodically, I would run into Mr. Sackler and he would say, "Too bad you weren't here yesterday, Mark was in. I looked for you."

And I would say, "Yeah, too bad."

But then one Friday I had just walked over to work to pick up my paycheck and I ran into Mr. Sackler in the parking lot.

"It's too bad you missed my son. He's going off to Denver to work for Atlantic Records at the end of this week."

"Oh, well, I'm sorry." The sun was shining and I was wearing a short blue jean skirt and a blue jean jacket held together with safety pins and decorated with religious medals, and lots of pink and blue necklaces.

"Hey," he looked surprised. "What're you doing tonight?"

"Nothing." I was even more surprised at my response.

"Why don't you come to the Hungry Bear at nine o'clock and I'll introduce you?"

"Okay."

The entire rest of the day I worried about what I had gotten myself into.

My cousin Dirk had to drive me because I hadn't yet gotten a car. Our habit was to go out every Friday night anyway, hitting all the gay and college bars, staying at each one for about five minutes. I was grateful that he found me cool enough to hang out with.

At about nine-fifteen we arrived and Mr. Sackler was waiting for us at the door. Dirk was obviously not happy. The Hungry Bear was a yuppie disco.

The three of us walked in and sat at a glass-topped table with white iron patio furniture chairs. Mr. Sackler told the pretty waitress to tell Mark we were there. She looked at us funny.

"He's very popular with all the women," Mr. Sackler explained.

After a few minutes, Mark bounded over. He was slim with short dark hair. Very good-looking and very young. Right after he met me he sat down. A skinny blonde walked by. "Hi Mar-ark," she said in that tone stupid girls use to indicate that you won't have to beg too hard to get them to sleep with you.

I raised my eyebrows at Dirk. It wasn't that easy to converse, the Strawberry Zots were playing in the next room.

Mr. Sackler had introduced us, then turned to talk to Dirk. That alone made me nervous. Mark was bouncing his leg. I wanted to pat it and tell him not to worry, he was about two thousand years too young for me. Instead I asked him about being a DJ.

"Great work, huh?"

"Yeah," he nodded his head several times. "Yeah, it is."

"What do you do afterward? I mean, aren't you all speeded up when you get off at three in the morning?"

"I watch movies."

"Oh yeah?" That interested me. Wilbur and I used to watch a lot of movies. "What kind of movies?"

"*Not that kind of movies!*"

I was startled. Heaven knows, the last thing I had been implying was that he watched porno movies. Evidently he did.

We both looked away in embarrassment.

He forgot and looked back at me, started singing along with the band. "G...L...O...R...I...A...A...A...A... Gloria. She wraps her hair round my legs, Gloria."

Jesus. He was looking right at me. I had to ask Dirk a question. Under the cover of the music I said, "Do you think we could gracefully leave in about thirty seconds?"

Dirk smiled wickedly. "Yeah. I think so. Whatever you want."

I turned back. Mark looked at me. He was very handsome.

"Well, I better get back to work," he said.

"Okay."

He got up and ran off. Dirk and I said polite good-byes to his father and were off, out the door in seconds.

Is It Really Possible There Could Be More to the Story, Right as It Is, in the Middle of Another Story

After that night at the Hungry Bear, I worked at the country club for another two years. Once, about a year later, an extremely good-looking guy came up to me.

"Hi, remember me?"

And to tell the truth, absolutely for the life of me, I had no idea who it was. Not even the tiniest inkling from which to make a guess.

"Mark, Mark Sackler."

"Oh, yeah." I looked down and ineffectually smoothed the skirt of my blue polyester uniform.

Then another year after that, the exact same thing. "Hi, remember me?"

And I swear these are the only two times this has ever happened to me in my life, but again, I hadn't a glimmer. Best to tell the truth.

"I'm sorry, but no, I don't . . ."

"Mark, Mark Sackler."

"Oh, yes, hi. Of course I remember you."

"I'm opening a club next Saturday. You should come."

"Wow, that's great. I'd love to, but I'm moving to New York City on Tuesday."

"Oh."

I knew I had been malicious. I wanted to get back at Albuquerque for all the imagined slights, waiting tables at the country club and no one ever bothering to find out that maybe I might be interesting, maybe I might have something to say. I was angry about Andy Hebenstriet being too afraid to even talk to me, and how hard I had to work to get Freddie to like me again, and even then it was all fucked up. I was happy now to be the one rejecting them.

Meantime, Back in the Present

Mark had smiled good-bye and left. His father leaned closer to me.

"All right, I have to go now. Are you sure you won't come watch a little TV?"

That was the thing men had, they were so persistent and they asked uncomplicated questions. They made it so easy for you to say yes. I couldn't seduce men that way. If I liked a guy I couldn't pretend like it was no big deal and make it cool for him to come home with me.

"What's your phone number?" He leaned toward me and slightly tilted his head for me to just say it in his ear.

"247-9671." What in the fuck was I doing giving him my phone number? I swear I will be eighty and some ninety-year-old, completely smug that he can still get a hard-on, will try to rape me, and I'll apologize for being uncooperative.

"Okay. I'm going to go now," Mr. Sackler said again.

"All right, bye, nice to talk to you."

I Miss Helen Almost Immediately

"How's it goin'?"
"Pretty good. I'm getting the book done. Though I don't know if New Mexico was the right place for work. I know too many people. It's better if I'm in a completely new place and I don't have anyone to talk to."

"Are you having fun?" Helen asked.

"Pretty much. How's stuff there?"

"The same. Darrin is of course torturing me and driving me crazy."

"Yeah, I like some guys here, but if I got close to them it'd be the same thing. Not like I don't know, of course I fucking know. I swear, I can spot someone from across the room: 'Oh yeah, his mother was crazy, his father drank and was withdrawn, we'll get along great.' I don't even have to meet them to know."

Helen said, "Hey June, I better go now. Is it okay if I call you tomorrow?"

Mark Sackler

"Can I buy you a shot?" he asked.

"No, thank you." I paused. I was wondering if I should make some remark about why I didn't want one. "No, thank you," I repeated. I felt like an idiot.

He looked surprised. I walked away. Fuck, I'd fucked up. I started dancing. Why didn't I accept? Maybe it would be okay to get drunk with him. Nah, I was way too crazy to drink. But maybe this time it would be okay. I had loved the whole thing of taking drugs and drinking where if you wanted someone all you had to do was ask them if they wanted to get high and the next thing you knew it was three weeks later and you were still sleeping in their bed.

A Million Boyfriends Is the Same as None at All

"Hi Helen."
"How's it going June?"

"Pretty good." That's what I always said. "I don't seem to be having any luck with the beautiful young boys at my club."

"Oh yeah? Why not do you think?"

"My new idea is to just do the most romantic thing possible. And it scares these guys. It occurs to me that it's possible that everyone is scared. And I can't have another boyfriend who's afraid. I need someone with no barriers where the energy can just flow back and forth unobstructed. You know, when you are in love with someone they are a mirror and you believe what they think of you. Like with Wilbur—because I knew he thought I was the hottest thing on two feet, I could do anything. I could see how he felt. When I walked into the room he would light up as if a switch had been thrown on inside him and that's how I felt about him too. Because of that I could take any risk, because I was already safe, I already knew how the person I cared the most about felt about me."

"I miss you, June. Why don't you come back tomorrow?"

I laughed. "Yeah, I should. I miss you too. I didn't realize how much I would."

"You'd hate it here though. The city is completely and disgustingly hot. Even Coney Island cannot be borne."

I laughed.

"So tell me more stuff." Helen said. "Let's stay on the phone for a really really long time."

"How's the movie?"

"Well, I'm taking an editing class. It started this week, so maybe I can learn that thing. And I put it on video because everyone said it'd be easier to do that way. I told you the footage is great. You look great. Though actually it seems to be a movie about your elbow. There are an amazing amount of shots of your elbow."

"What else?"

"I'm going to Buffalo next weekend to see my friend Charles. I told you about him. He is so beautiful. He is so thin and his skin is transparent. When he takes his shirt off you can see his heart beating. Sometimes I have sex with him."

"I'm jealous. I never get to have sex."

"Maybe that's good."

"Yeah, you're right. I swear, you know, the thing about having sex—if I do it with the wrong person I get depressed. It took me years to figure this out because I'm so dumb. Like speed. It took me a while with that too. Like yeah, I'd feel great, but then wouldn't know why I was depressed for three weeks afterwards. But do you think we talk about sex too much?"

Helen laughed. "What else would we talk about? Art? I think we allot art as much time as it deserves."

"What about food?"

"Food is great."

"Okay, how about, umm—are there any subjects left? Mothers?" I suggested facetiously.

"That leads right back to sex, doesn't it?" Helen was using her gravelly, the words just barely making it out of her mouth, sex voice.

"Hey, what about metaphysics?"

"Is that the same as love?"

"Yeah. Love of a person is. Love of a concept is the rest of science."

"I think love of a person is just a door. It's the thing of, you are madly in love with someone, so much that you love the bad things about them as much as the good things. You know, the way I feel about Derhead. And it's just a metaphor, just a learning tool for you to figure out how to feel that way about everyone."

I laughed. "Brilliant. I remember the first time I really figured out I was connected to everyone. It was here. I used to hang out at the bus station because it was near my house, and they had a video jukebox with a lot of different stuff on it. Guns N' Roses and Madonna and also Ella Fitzgerald and Duke Ellington. I think they had turned some old movie or early TV footage into videos of them. Anyway, I was thinking about what I would most like to happen after I died and it occurred to me that I could be a multi-sided crystal and on each side be having some sort of exchange, you know, like the one we're having now, and then I thought, what if I got bored? So if that happened, I could just reinvent a world in which I was everyone, like I would be the bank robbers and rapists as well as the diplomats and beauty queens, the Brazilian housewives with five children."

"Yeah?"

"Well you know, then I thought maybe that's already happening, maybe everyone is me, and I suddenly got this intense conviction that that was true and I looked around and of course, what I saw were people in the bus station."

Helen laughed.

"Didn't make it less true."

She laughed again. "Hey, did I tell you I sent everyone a thank-you note for being in the movie?"

"Great."

"I thought you might want to hear the messages they left on my answering machine tape, so I turned it over and I'm saving it for when you get back."

"Wow. Thanks."

104

"Yeah." She knew that'd make me happy.

"So what time is it there?"

"Ten million o'clock." Helen sounded like a sleepy kid.

"Okay."

"I'll call again."

"Yeah, okay. I love you. Bye."